Dick Wimmer's short stories have appeared in literary magazines, and he has collaborated with Bob Reiner on a Movie-of-the-Week entitled *The Million Dollar Infield*. His book *Baseball Fathers, Baseball Sons* was published in the USA in 1988. Dick Wimmer also teaches Creative Writing. He lives in Agoura, California.

Dick Wimmer

IRISH WINE

published by Pan Books

First published in the United States of America in 1988 by
Mercury House, San Francisco, California
This Picador edition first published in Great Britain in 1988 by
Pan Books Ltd, Cavaye Place, London SW10 9PG
9 8 7 6 5 4 3 2 1
© Dick Wimmer 1988

ISBN 0 330 30881 5

Printed and bound in Great Britain by
Cox & Wyman Ltd, Reading, Berkshire

For lovely Vicki,
"the secret place where I am really I"

Boyne

"*CRAZY!* Good God, Turner, this is *CRAZY*—absolutely *CRAZY*—finally having my life come down to me parked across these railroad tracks by a stormy, surging Irish Sea, lightning bolts streaking the sky, in the green Jaguar sedan with the canoe still atop it—Bach's 'Sleepers Awake' booming out over my tapedeck (E.Power Biggs on the organ)—gargling down this last bottle of Irish wine, drunk blissfully out of my mind, and waiting for the train from Kilcoole to come roaring round the bend and end it all with a bang!

"I mean just *LOOK* at me, Billy, seven bloody years after conquering the whole of London's art world, 'the most promising painter of his generation,' I'm broke, bereft, and totally *forgotten*, 3 pounds 6 in my pocket, my patron Sligo (so dismayed by my upcoming show?) blowing his brains out a month ago today and now they're taking my *daughter* away (stealing her from me, I should say!), so what the hell's *LEFT* to live for?"—a cascading cloudburst wildly lashing the glass, more flashes of jagged lightning across Erin's green and fragrant shore— "Though soon we'll be together at last, you, the greatest painter of the nineteenth century, Joseph Mallord 'Billy' Turner, and I, the greatest painter of the twentieth, Seamus Eamon Boyne!

1

'Cause they were *ALWAYS* out to get me, never giving us our due, having killed off Van Gogh, Cézanne, Gauguin, and Modigliani or calling me 'a sheer pornographer'! All those agonizing struggles to seize my blazing visions and pin 'em down, wasted, gone astray—But Christ, what the hell's it matter anyway? Might as well ascend with this torrential shower thundering in my ears and these long tapering fingers (that still hold as much talent as you) trilling my grizzled beard!

"For Good *God*, just *LOOK* at that patrician's face, of regal grace, and that glazed yet piercing royal blue gaze staring back from my rearview mirror! Thirty-eight-year-old comfortably rumpled Boyne in his red hooded sweatshirt, slightly frayed, and the cant of his dashing beret!—time fading, my wine draining, Billy—and this gray rain still insanely splashing across my Jaguar sedan and canoe strapped to the silver roof rack—seven years driving around Ireland this way while those Yahoos jeered 'the eccentric painter' out to play, Boyne the blusterer, the artist manqué!

"Though what'd those whorish critics once say: 'A remarkably gifted original,' 'Far ahead of his time'? Compared initially to you, Billy, then ignoring me in my prime—as only *Hagar*, dearest friend of mine (just wiring him that farewell note: 'By the time you read this I'll be dead'), truly understood! Starting me painting again right after Laura'd left when I produced the finest works of my life: those early 'pornographic nudes' aswhirl in a fluttering vortex of light! Show after disastrous show and the one tomorrow night that the critics'll surely pan—*O Jesus*, those bastards driving me *MAD!!*" tears suddenly streaming out of my eyes, flinging this wine behind me, "Sons of *bitches*, bloodsucking *queers*—and now *NOTHING* left to live for: no daughter, wife, friends, or life, and the public couldn't care *less* as I've grown 'distinctly out of favor,' Yahoos Warhol and Bacon still the rage, reaching the end of my tether! Laura in Baltimore with her wealthy Jewish lawyer and Tory, my girl, whom she's trying to deny me from *ever* seeing!

"God*damn* you, Laura, you avenging *BITCH*, you just had to twist the knife, last straw, that pushed me over the edge—"

"Zounds, lad, no NEED to kill yourself now!" Turner's gruff London basso sounding in my ears, **"For I've seen your work and it's no doubt the finest since my own nearly 120 years ago! So never you mind — they called my *Snow Storm* 'a mass of soapsuds and whitewash,' brought tears to my very eyes — for NONE of 'em are going to beat you again!! A final laugh, lad, you'll have your revenge!"** "Yes, but how do I *achieve* it now, an artist's lasting fame, recognized as the genius I've always been — ?" **"Precisely! and hang forever in the Tate beside me! There's a marvelous spot on the wall nearby, be just right for you!"** "O Mother of Christ, what if it could be? Sligo a trustee! Just get *one* of my paintings hung and my struggles would all be *worth* it — "

　　WHEEEEEEE!!!

　　GOOD GOD! and here comes that bloody Kilcoole train *roaring* round the bend, its whistle loudly wailing —

　　"Wait, wait, can't die *now,* have to get out of here and hang in the Tate beside you!!" Starting my car — trying to start my car — O *Jesus,* not *now,* not *NOW!* Come on, come on! Stereo running too long, Bach still booming, big bang looming — the train bearing down, shrilling its whistle again, making my beard stand on end — *CRASH!!* Mary and Joseph, the back window's shattering glass! A *shotgun* blast? Aiming at me? But why? No one even knows I'm *alive! —* The Jag *finally* turning over and jamming my foot to the floor as I go careening forward with a screech of spinning tires, bumping and bouncing over these teeth-rattling tracks and on through this thundering rain with that monstrous train filling the rearview mirror and — *Suffering Christ! ANOTHER* gunshot knocking my canoe clear off — as I keep speeding along past dripping hedgerows, blurry fields of grass and hay, and that surging Irish Sea —

　　"O get off my *arse,* you blasted train, bloody assassin, 'cause *no one's* going to kill me *NOW!!!"*

Hagar

Screeching up before our Long Island City office, *Hagar Pest Control* above that blinking neon roach, and hurrying through the metal door past the tan plastic paneling, my father's picture on the wall — already haggard two years ago, a round-shouldered Ralph Bellamy with distinguished graying temples, raccoon squint and double chin — by chemical company calendars, insect photos, and my mother with her new blonde perm and gold-rimmed glasses with their beaded chains — plumply seated at the front desk, tamping out her Chesterfield and talking on the phone.

"—O sure, I know it takes time to adjust but I just hate staying alone, so I come home, I cry, I empty my stomach from nervous cramps, then I take a pill to relax — *Who's there?* O Gene! God, you scared me! See, like I told you, Mrs. Shish, perfect timing, my son *just* walked in! Yeah, so listen, Mrs. — yeah, I'll have him call you right — no-no, right back, right — " raising her eyes to the fluorescent lights and shaking her head, pushing the ashtray aside, "O no more than five minutes, tops, as soon as he gets his bearings. Sure, sure, of course, of course, bye-bye," and hanging up, "*Oi gottenyu!* Your friend Shish from your softball playing, his mother, the beauty, lives in Great Neck Estates, pays Harder $5 a month, says she only wants to talk to the boss, so maybe you can meet Herman there at three?"

"Yeah, yeah, well we'll see," sitting down at this cluttered desk and leaning forward on the edge of my chair with my eyelid twitching away.

"And how come you're late? You feel all right?"

"I'm fine, fine, I just didn't get much sleep last night."

"You're still carrying on over that *meshuggener* from Ireland?"

"I've been trying to reach him—"

"Running around like a chicken with your head cut off, don't sleep, don't eat—"

"Ma—"

"Who in his right mind sends a telegram like that? And whatta you hear from Teri?"

"Nothing."

"Nothing! But she's still in North Dakota? O God, crazy altogether! Some *facocktah* wife—"

"Ma, just forget it, will you!" The phone ringing.

"And look at your eye! How long's your eye been twitching like that? Wait just a minute, let me get this," placing her Chesterfield in the ashtray, "Hagar Pest. What? O, hold it. Gene do we do bats?"

Blinking and glancing over, "No. Where are they?"

"Northport."

"No, it's a nuisance, let them get somebody local there." She hanging up. "Yeah, so what else is happening?"

"What else? I'm workin' like a dog, just one after another, and Nick is on vacation, Rodriquez took the whole weekend off that he wasn't entitled to, three other men are out sick, and we're getting so much business now."

Loosening my tie and arranging my calls in order beside this stack of mail, "What, termites?"

"No, the other stuff, roaches, rats, bees, fleas, everything— and I'm all alone here, getting a beautiful cold," daubing her nose with a tissue, then lighting up another Chesterfield.

"Where's the girl you hired to help you?"

"She didn't come in today, so I'm knockin' my brains out. All the work on her desk, the accountants're coming in Tuesday, and all those termite inspections to make — always at the end of the month, you know, so we'll have to date back a few days."

"Yeah, well listen, Ma, before I forget, did you hear anything else about that offer to buy the business?"

"O come on, it could take forever! They have to consult with their lawyers, their accountants, God knows who — they all want something for nothing! Your father, may he rest in peace, built up this entire business himself without a penny — " The phone ringing again.

"Hold on, I'll get it. Hagar Pest. Santoro, right, go: 25 for the service call and $5 a month. Fine, bye," then back to my mother, "So what were you saying about that part-time girl, why isn't she working?"

"O nothing, nothing," and taking a final puff, she tamps out her cigarette in the glass ashtray, "We had a fight."

"Fight? What kind of fight?"

"Who knows! She got annoyed, said she wasn't coming in today, says she wants to talk to you."

"Talk to *me?*"

"Yeah," smiling as she keeps on tamping, "says she likes you, feels you understand her. So *you* talk to her, whatever good it'll do — " The phone ringing again.

"OK, OK, I'll talk to her. Hagar Pest. Yeah, White Plains, go: 50 and 8 — "

"She's got a terrific deal here for herself. Where else is she gonna go home in the middle of the afternoon? But that's the kind of help you get nowadays."

"OK, OK, I said I'll *talk* to her!"

"Your father, may he rest in peace, should only know, he would've thrown her out one-two-three and that'd be that!"

"Yeah, well I'm *not* my father — " All the phones now ringing at once. "Hagar Pest. Right, Herman, that job in Roslyn, OK? You quoted her $40 and she'll call tomorrow. How much guarantee? Sixty days. How is it, bad? Right, anyway — Hello? — O I thought we got cut off, 'cause this place is really a madhouse now, I just walked in and I've gotta get outta here, I'm already late as it is — O and Herman, listen, I got one in Great Neck Estates, a

Mrs. Shish on Deepdale. Right, 42 Deepdale, so I'll meet you there at three, fine, bye."

My mother lighting up another Chesterfield as she talks on her line, and turning to me, "They towed you away? How could they possibly —?"

"What's going on *now?*"

"Just a minute, hold the wire," as she cups her hand over the phone, "Roger, the colored fellow, was parked on Madison Avenue and Sixty-third Street and they towed his car away."

"What was he parked *there* for?"

"Well he was doing a job around the corner, cop told him to watch it, so they towed him away. Costs $50."

"Fantastic!" standing — all my papers scattering over the floor.

"And Mastro got mugged in the Bronx last night —"

"Wait a second, wait a second, take it easy, *Christ,* one at a time!" hearing my father's voice in mine, "Is Mastro on the line?"

"No, no, I talked to him before but he's better now. O and that one from August came through on yours, that Chock Full O' Nuts —"

"OK, OK, fine," gathering all my calls together.

" — then I took one this morning, Gene, just before you came in, out in Huntington, has carpet beetle larvae and I told her you'd take a look at it this afternoon and there's another in —"

"All right, *enough,* will you, let me get *out* of here already!"

"OK, OK, but wait just a second, Gene, before you leave, I've gotta run to the bathroom now, empty myself out again, so just stay a minute longer to answer the phones and I'll be right back," and she goes rushing up the stairs.

Riffling through this stack of mail, bills, payments, Pest Control Conference in Amherst, Mass. — as I keep rubbing my fluttering eyelid — and Boyne *can't* be dead! No way! Still madly jigging in my memory, with his beard and beret, wildly swaying to that Irish reel, and into the dance I went, gathering momentum, heel and toe, do-si-do, feet flicking, kicking out, and my mind zigzagging as we spun about — a massive wave crashing in, swallowing him up, he dying, our dream dying, have to get to him in time!

Seven years gone by—Carnaween in that summer of 1960: our mad, whirlwind spree, Boyne's twelve-room house by the Irish Sea, Delgany, County Wicklow, Ireland. He who persuaded me to write and forsake my father's world on that first trip to Europe when I was twenty-four and the wash and wear I wore as I fled New York with Joyce in my teeming brain and writing somewhere, who knew, out there to find, and I found Boyne and Dublin and Ciara, my blonde poetic dream (before I was black-mailed home!): our first time alone, her hair of Scandinavian shine as she moved around that houseboat on the Seine in her purple robe—and I moved too, tumbling her waywardly onto their bed, "—*No,* Gene, I have to wash and dress if you still want to go to the Louvre—" the firm crease of her spine as I kept widening the purple silk—"Please, leave it alone, stop playing—O all *right!*" and flipping open the robe to reveal her high breasts, hips, and fleece before shutting the sight with a silent slam, muscular dents in her calves as she swept into the bathroom and closed the door—then soon reappeared with her hair slightly damp, holding a dripping brush, "Just you keep still for a while!" serious, looking down her nose, "I cannot possibly love you yet, I hardly know you," her ripe rump shifting as she brushed out the shine, "God, still so dirty and I just washed it!" "It looks grand to me, *seraphically* filthy!" "O you and your blonde hair!" and spinning about with impish eyes, she hopped onto the bed, fanning her hair over my surprise, her robe flopping open and hastily shed from those kindling curves I just couldn't stop feeling as I buried my head between her thighs—

The phone stridently ringing!—Jesus, *now* what? Some crazy customer with a cockroach in his bed? "Hagar Pest, hello? Hello?" The sound of breathless panting. "Anybody there? *Hello? What* is this, an obscene phone call? Maybe you should talk to my mother?"

"Good *God,* Gene, that has to be you!"

"And who the hell's—*BOYNE?* You're *ALIVE!!* How the hell *are* you, *where* the hell are you, and what the hell's going on, sending me that *telegram?*"

"O bit of a hullabaloo, being pursued by killers and choo-choos—and somebody just took a shot at me!"

"At *you?* But who? Why?"

"Haven't got a bloody clue! *Suffering Christ*, you can't even kill yourself in peace anymore without someone trying to do it for you!"

"But where are you now, still in—?

"Where am *I?* O I'm *all* over, Hagar, in the sea, the air, the clouds—there's no place I'm not! I'm matter, pure matter—Jesus, I'm *what* matters in this insane zoo of a world! But how the blazes are you, tell me how you are? You have a wifey yet, that dream girl of your past, Dutch colleen?"

"No—you never met her."

"I see, but a wifey nonetheless? And what's she do, doing to you?"

"She just left me."

"Ah right, off on a spree! Well *my* wife's stealing my daughter from me!"

"Stealing your daughter?"

"O no way she'll ever succeed, just get *one* of my paintings hung in the Tate and my struggles will all be worth it!"

"Yeah, well how'd you get this number, called my home, my parents—?"

"No, no, left Da-da alone."

"My father just died, two months ago—"

"Ah, Mother of Christ! sorry to hear that now, never met him but I felt I knew him."

"And I've been calling Ireland God knows *how* many times since I got your note, trying to find you but you had no phone, weren't listed—"

"Well here I bloody well am in this Irish booth, calling the reigning King of the Cockroach World to tell him I'm having another show, my Comeback Show, the greatest show of my career, so you have to come over *now*, Hagar, *tomorrow*, only one left I can count on, the two of us *together* again in this moment of dire need—and we'll stay in Kew, Dungannon's cottage, no one suspect us there!"

"*Tomorrow?* Well hold it, you still haven't told me—wait a second, I mean, Jesus, how can I just take off?"

"You just get on a plane and go! 'Cause this is the last chance for me and a *second* chance for you to recapture the past before you're engulfed *forever* in that bug business—and I knew you'd come through, could *always* count on you—"

"Seamus, no—"

My mother coming back down the stairs, "*Oi gottenyu*, took another pill to relax—Who's that? Who're you yelling at?"

"—or take a cab from Heathrow, fastest way, to Tattersall Wharf in Kew and—*Good God!* somebody's coming, have to go! I'll see you tomorrow, Gene, God bless!"

"Seamus—?" The rattling clank of his phone—with my eyelid really twitching away.

"Gene, what's going on, what's the matter, *who* was that?"

"My friend in Ireland."

"Now he's alive, the *meshuggener?* I thought he was dead!"

Boyne

Slinking swiftly by my greenhouse with the rain still pummeling and slashing down and on through the vestibule — the front door locked. *LOCKED?* O Suffering *Christ,* locked it before I left, never planning to return — and Hagar'll soon be over — with me out here all day in this endless Irish shower, sopping wet grass, waiting to be picked off by some IRA marksman, crazed creditor, purblind hunter, Laura's hit man — my battered Jag safely out of sight after I came hurtling off the tracks over that low retaining wall, the canoe a splintered mass! Smash in these windows? My waterlogged reflection on the drizzled glass, while out here, gray sheets of rain bucketing over my beret and grizzled beard, I sip the streaming drops and slip deftly through these hedges, odd laurel and sodden yew, to look in at my studio —

Ah, *this* window's slightly open! Gusts fluttering the tattered drapes and up with this splattered sash, onto the ledge — and *plunk!* — into the cluttered room. Guinness bottles glittering as I slosh past half-finished canvases, easels, my ancient organ by the wall, and briskly down the hall toward the kitchen, dusty motes pollinating the air, alone again in this cold house by a stormy sea — nobody here but my paints and me? — and over the cracked black tile of the kitchen.

11

Rummaging frantically through all these cabinets filled
with empty tins of Danoxa Irish Stew, Birds Eye Minceburgers,
Buitoni Canelloni as I wolf down this stale pile of crumbs and
slivers of moldy cheese — so ravenous after fear! Just pass it off as
an errant shot or definite sinister deed? 'Cause who the hell
knows I *exist* anymore, grovelling for my daily bread? — "Though
soon, Billy, there'll be wine, food, and wonders *galore* before we
reach Jerusalem!" — then scurry wetly up the stairs, over this
once-varnished floor to my unmade rumpled bed, green sheets
in need of a wash — green from mold or their natural verdant
color? God only knows anymore! Lived up here off the frozen
food with newspapers up to my chin, my sterno stove placed
upon my chest, a pot of boiling water and popped 'em right in —
no mess, no fuss, I never left the bed! Ah, and here are my
sunglasses under these musty socks and towels. Cleaning 'em off
and fitting 'em on — and let's see, what disguise should I wear to
go meet Sligo's daughters? Something funereal? My raveling
Claddagh sweater for the warmth that's in it, dashing black beret,
and this yellow slicker from my seafaring days: I'll go as the
Ancient Mariner — who soon'll be displayed in the Tate!

Toward this dark chilly loo, past the mirror as my eyes come
into focus, to unleash a long arching pee — setting a new Olympic record for tapping a kidney as these last drops dribble down.
And what did poor Sligo say last time I saw him: *If you come visit
me again, Boyne, my only requirements are that you must have bathed
and are fulfilling your true potential* — and I haven't done either, not
having washed in weeks, months, or God knows when, odors
wearing themselves out! My water shut off yesterday: no heat,
light, gas, nor water, bubbling urine lying stagnant in the bowl,
can't even flush it down — so I'll pop into Dublin and sneak in a
bath — before paying my respects to those two crazy daughters of
Sligo-Moeran, living in their castle in Phoenix Park, where I'll
turn on the charm and tell 'em my plan!

The rain still falling, a steady, splattering pour as I come
trotting down the stairs and full speed out the door — an elusive,
moving target — round the greenhouse with its long slanted
panes, sprawled in there these last few days, my face to the sky,

gray colors filtering down and black despair filing me up—and the sea out there still cresting with whitecaps and gulls floating low, their wasp legs dangling, to sit upon the rocks and be rained on as over this rickety gate I go, splashing past the garage and my battered Jag.

Along Tobercurry Road and up these metal stairs, across the railroad bridge, my suicide spot way down there around that bend, the Irish accepting such shenanigans as the routine gesture of the avant-garde—fewer suicides in Ireland than anywhere else on earth—as the sun like a peeling tangerine in this lustrous air comes slowly peeking through, all these windows turning aqua-blue (assassins lurking behind them?), and down this narrow street, worn holes in my soles, and my sodden feet soaking up the wet—

"Ah, Mr. Boyne—" nearly leaping out of my shoes!

"—about yer bill, sir?"

O Mother of *Christ*, Dennehy, the bloody bartender, no shotgun in sight!

"Not Boyne—Apparition—Celtic ghost!" quickly heading the other way.

"Just that it's gotten out of hand, Mr. Boyne, been several months now—Watch *out*, man!!"

GOOD GOD!—a trio of massive lorries—another attempt? Who knows!—passing between us as I dodge nimbly across the road under this dark green awning, the savor of feety cheese, wasps swarming round the peaches and pears—fat pears, ripe shamefaced peaches—and briskly through this crowded shop, pesky flies buzzing all about, stalls heaped high with fruits and vegetables, comestibles, oranges, lemons, and Cavaillion melons—pressing and palping their shiny skins—and Dennehy still out there wiping the spray from his face and wondering where I went, could disappear without a trace: Houdini's alive and well and living in Ireland! And that elderly lady by the door complaining to Fanning the grocer, a bald walrus with his Turkish moustache, about the high cost of grapes nowadays as I continue fondling the peaches and pears and these ripe juicy pippins—small curves of sheen on their applegreen surface—

and swiftly under my slicker (refreshing change from my Minceburgers and moldy cheese), but the question still remaining: how the hell do I get *out* of here? as I filch another pear — last few farthings in my pocket and this linty Chiclet —

"Say, what the hell're ya *doin'* up there?" My heart violently pounding! "And what've you got under yer coat?"

"Coat? No, no, just a ratty old fisherman's sweater," shuffling a few steps back, "examining these fine fruits here —" as jowly Fanning with a raging scowl comes charging by the melons.

And narrowly missing the swipe of his paw as he chases me into the chemist's next door, spinning round and round these postcard racks — peekaboo — and out once again, Dennehy now joining the hullabaloo, and down this cobblestone alley beside the Fluff 'n' Fold Laundry, skipping across a back garden, trampling cabbages as I go — God, better off *killing* myself, for Christ's sake, or *being* killed, all my creditors coming out of the woodwork! — and a fast left toward this fancy entrance, sign above: "Pavlova Dance Institute, Class now in progress," the *Nutcracker Suite* —

And a few moments later soaring out the rear with a great Baryshnikov leap in a pink tutu and crown over my beret — the *grand jeté* carrying me into the kitchen of Wong Fat's Mongolian Barbecue reeking of monosodium glutamate and past that tall black chef slicing bamboo shoots and bellowing, "Hold the rice, baby!" as I breeze by the watercolor Buddhas — the restaurant empty, owner Wong Fat probably down in the cellar carving his Szechwan ribs — to a small corner table and this bowl of dry noodles! panting as I munch 'em down and fluff out my tutu — my slicker back with Pavlova's *corps de ballet* (through shrieking, tulle, and that Tchaikovsky Suite!) — So damned famished now, my heart still pounding away! used to come here often during the winter to observe Mongolian food on display: the pale green of snowpeas and succulent peppers a scarlet red, all the while wolfing down these free noodles, then pretending to order two from column A before shaking my head and leaving — till Wong Fat chased me out with a cleaver —

SLAM! The doors to the kitchen crashing open and Wong Fat, looking like a ferocious little Buddha with gleaming cleaver in hand, "You-you, you clazy man," making a beeline straight for me, "now I gonna *keel* you!"

Knocking over this table in my haste and scattering dry noodles all over the place, apples and pears bounding by me as I burst out the door, sprinting through these puddles round the corner — and O Jesus, there goes the bus to Dublin!

Signalling and frantically waving it down in my pink tutu and crown — Wong Fat, Fanning, and Dennehy now joined in hot pursuit, the *corps de ballet* behind them — a kindly ballerina tossing me my slicker as I scramble aboard, grabbing onto this door — and the bus goes roaring off up the hill, a blur of them back there fading in our wake!

"Ah, turned out to be a grand mornin', didn't it, sir?" The driver just smiling without dismay, eccentric painter out to play, " — Yes, grand, grand — " taking off my crown and hooking it — "O sorry, madam, sorry" — in this woman's hair, prunish face of a Pekingese, "Here, let me just free these — " her blonde hair rising up from her scalp — Good *God*, it's a *wig!* and she's bald as a billiard ball! The woman screaming and pounding me with her umbrella. "Madam, I'm terrible sorry — " The bus bouncing, swerving — Christ, we're going over this goddamn cliff, tumble down Bray Head into the sea! And she's still hitting me — Only one thing to do: chewing my Chiclet a couple of times, "Here, madam, this should work," and pressing it first to the wig, then onto her scalp — the woman screaming even louder now, "Mother of Jaysus, please let me *out* of here!!" as she rushes off at the next screeching stop, holding her lopsided hair, and the whole bus laughing as we go bouncing away.

Down, down to Dublin on the Stillorgan Road, by the tulip blossom and thyme and Booterstown sign — Lautrec's father wearing a tutu to dinner in lieu of a kilt — and all these Irish eyes smiling at me as I take this seat in the rear between gaunt rawboned features and decaying yellow teeth, and the whole bus, including the driver, crossing themselves en masse as we go rattling past that Gothic church down the long curving hill, old women with black shawls and hobnail boots and the girls with windy hair waiting by the queues for buses of another number, the signs for Milltown and Ranelagh — and "*Guinness*," reads that clattering truck, "*is Good for you*" — and Good *God*, I agree, could really use one now!

"'Cause you see, Billy, what I have to put up with? Every great artist *hounded* in his time and widely misunderstood! When I ventured even further into a riot of color and light, they called me mad and dismissed as disasters my subsequent shows as quickly as they'd once honored and praised the first one! Vilified and ridiculed, and labelling all my old work 'sheer pornography,' 'sinking to lurid sensuality,' insinuating I was suffering from some *mental* disease! Tears, too, in my eyes as I read those reviews — but Billy, the hell with that now 'cause *ONE* work's all I need to hang in the Tate beside you!"

And what a marvelous face that woman has over there, looking like an ostrich about to bury her head in the sand — no chin below her slender beak and bloated eyes — and staring straight ahead as though she hasn't seen or heard a word I've said. Love to give her a gentle pet, then do her in gay pastels! But I still haven't had my bath as yet, so I'll try some Dublin hotels — if I ever survive this morning!

On down deeper into the city toward Ballsbridge and the Royal Canal, that policeman out there with his white baton and three-quarter-length gauntlets directing traffic across those wide blocks of zebra stripe, past gold nameplates, black spoke fences, and the fanlights of clear polished glass, Merrion Square, Clare, and the back gates of Trinity, with a flock of students scurrying to class and the soft wet grass glistening in the sun as we sweep by Westland Row under the Loop Line Bridge and left toward the Abbey, Pearse, and College Street, the Trinity railings where the bus pulls to the side of the road and I hop off with an agile bound — donating my tutu and crown to the driver!

And round this madding crowd and the Dublin of today, fitting back on my slicker, sunglasses, and the black beret, toward Dawson Street and the massive Royal Hibernian where I'll have me a proper shower!

Spinning up the elegant steps of this veddy, veddy English hotel with the doorman bowing and across the high-ceilinged lobby with its pale blue draperies, a pair of wrinkled-jowled dowagers glancing over through ducal lorgnettes from their wicker chairs as I nip up the back stairs to the first floor landing and I'll give that room a try — Rap-rap: "Yes?" "O sorry, wrong room" — and off the other way, following these stairs to the top, over the polished runners and green floral patterns, and down the end of that hall and open door — looking in, no one about, probably just checked out — Yes or no? Never any doubt as I ease it softly shut.

Tell the char I just popped back for an urgent pee, had to tap a kidney — and Suffering *Christ,* will you just *look* at that desecration on the wall: these apples appearing as plastic fruit! Still life print of Cézanne's, who once said, "With an apple I will astonish Paris." And prints of my own work much the same, never coming *close* to the seething heart of the color, pressing 'em out all joyless and flat like Turner seen through gauze, with little left of the coarse and lumpy, pulsing lovely gleam of the paint! And shedding this yellow slicker now and the rest of my clothes as I skip on into the shower.

Right, all the essentials here, pink bars of soap, reams of towels — and my heart still resounding with fear, keeping the demons at bay! Someone come busting through that door to expose me in the raw or drill me full of holes, bump me off, rub me out, expunge me from the face of Erin's green and fragrant shore: the finest painter of the twentieth century who'll soon be enshrined in the Tate! The shower's warm spray ricocheting off my bald dome as I keep gargling and spewing gleefully away, now crooning Bach's "Sleepers Awake"!

"Both of us, Billy, needing water and coastlines to stimulate our work: your beloved Thames and my Irish Sea or childhood's Hudson River! For I am my work, as Courbet said, even part of the composition — caressing my handprints over the canvas — however long I may live! Everyone dying around me — and still so shaken by Sligo's death (now Hagar's father), hiding out in the bogs of incognito — For Billy, yours was a barber and devoted

friend who hung your early works round his shop and mine was
a short-order chef who thought he was Escoffier incarnate!
Crazed with grandiose dreams by the sauces he'd invented, he
strove toward immortality and went mad for never attaining it:
dear Timothy Patrick Boyne, sweet father of mine, from Valhalla,
New York, who died—*Jesus!* in that private asylum—and my
mother, Aideen, from Glengariff, who dabbled in watercolors
and guided me through my first museums—till driven up the
wall by poor Tim, she finally deserted him when I was nine!"

And now for this pink sweet-smelling soap, circular
motions around the wool of my prime, across my middle, and
down my thighs—could use a little meat on these wasted bones,
must be twenty pounds underweight—and pausing to rest in
soapy foam, watching the hot droplets race down the tile, one in
particular as it wends its way in a serpentine rimple—now caught
and destroyed in the gust of a splash (like that Kilcoole train
smashing me flat, shotgun searing my brain, this shower never
occurring!)—and Hagar, dear friend (exterminator's son thinking he's James Joyce), and I soon together again as I rinse fresh
and clean and turn off the taps—A *voice* from the other room?

"—Ah yes, t'irty-foyve years oyve been here the Hoybernian,
rabbi."

Who the hell is *THAT?*

"Well that's marvelous and thank you so very much. This is
for you."

"Ah, that's grand. And if there's anythin' else you'll be
wantin', sir, just give us a shout."

GOOD GOD, and there's no way *out!* Sure to come in
here—So what do I do, just walk on through? Hear them
puttering around outside, English rabbi and his wife, muttering
and unpacking—Just frolic in nude and welcome 'em to Ireland
or claim I'm an *Irish* rabbi and that it's *my* bloody room? Be in
here soon, have to beat 'em to the punch, with the element of
surprise!

Patting myself dry and holding onto these clothes and small
paunch of underwear—and what'll I say? No idea.

Just a deep breath as I appear, grinning in my birthday suit, before their dumfounded stares, and closing this blue door behind me.

Not a sound, exhaling as I look around and down the empty hall, my nape hair wildly splayed—

O Mother of *Christ*, forgot my beret! *Have* to have it, *can't* live with out it—Only one thing to do, heart still pounding, spinning about.

Knock-knock.

"Who's there?"

"Wet man!"

The door slowly opening as I saunter in with my chin held high toward the shower and my precious beret (probably assuming it's part of some ancient Irish custom or, like Gilbert and Sullivan, I'm the checker of the loo), and back through the room with the wife shyly nodding and—Good *God*, tipping me a shilling—as I flash bare-arsed out the door once more!

And down the carpeted stairs to slip struggling into my clothes, get these over the moist toes—there! mismatched socks, shirt, pants, the raveled Irish sweater, and yellow slicker that fell on the floor—my heels scuffing over these polished runners and across the high-ceilinged lobby with its pale blue draperies, my reflection gleaming in the passing glass: grizzled beard and the dashingly canted beret, the doorman still bowing and wishing me a good day as down the front steps I go, off now to Sligo's with my jiggling paunch of underwear, up the slope of Dawson Street—

"Look *out,* sir!"

—*O JESUS!!*

And a monstrously grinning gargoyle crashing at my feet!

Hagar

Aging Rose Shish loudly clacking through her vestibule with her tanned horsy face and brassy harridan hair, wearing a pink chenille housecoat and a pair of pomponed silver mules, "Well look who finally got here, took you long enough 'cause I'm nearly *hysterical* already with these waterbugs!"

O Christ, this is all I *need* today! following behind her and paunchy Herman in his Hagar Pest jacket and baggy brown denims —

"Been calling and calling — So go 'head and take care of them, will you please, figure *out* what you have to do and get them the hell out of here!"

"We'll do our best, Mrs. Shish —"

"You know I hardly sleep anymore, have no idea what I've been going through, my nerves so frazzled — Thank God for Valium!"

"Well just relax, Mrs. Shish, I'm here now and I'll go take a look —"

"And you're the *boss* now? Do the actual work with your jacket and tie on? You and my son Harry used to play together as *kids!*"

"Well you know, Mrs. Shish, what we do for special customers —"

"And I'm just so disgusted! I don't know what your mother told you, everything that happened, all the details?"

O *Jesus,* here it comes now! "Well only that—"

"I'd just got home from this bar mitzvah Sunday, eating like a pig—the Fingerhuts, I don't know if you know them, they live near Harry in Russell Gardens—and naturally I rushed right into that bathroom over there, the closest one I could find and—God, I don't even know if I can talk about it now, I get so nervous, palpitations! I mean ever since I was a little girl in Yonkers, the sight of a bug, even a little gnat or an ant, and here was this *enormous* black thing sitting right there on my toilet seat—"

It should've bit you in the ass! "I understand, Mrs. Shish—"

"—and I let out such a scream the neighbors must've thought someone was being murdered in here, and ran and called Harder and he sprayed, but this morning he, the bug I'm talking about now, was back again, except now there were two of them—he brought along his cousin, I suppose—"

"Mrs. Shish—?"

"—and Harder couldn't get here, some nonsense excuse, so I finally called you, spoke to your mother, this man came out—"

"Mrs. Shish, why don't I take a look—?"

"—and now I'm getting *hysterical* again!"

"Right, I know how frightening it can be," massaging my twitching eyelid—

"Last night I heard them in the attic, the cellar—"

"Well you don't have to worry anymore, Mrs. Shish, I'll take care of it—"

"—and it's worse now than it's ever been, twenty-six years I've lived here—I'm going to sell this damn house! Ever since Oscar, my late husband, passed away, I've been all alone by myself. Harry says I'm crazy living alone but what does he know, he never calls, never comes over anyway, I can't depend on him with his *goyisheh* wife, that *couveh* from the Five Towns—"

"Well I'll take a look downstairs—"

"Yeah, and listen, as long as you're here, I also saw these tiny little flying things in my closet, you know the kind, that flit around—?"

"Right, Herman'll be happy to check those out for you, Mrs. Shish."

"And you'll take care of the other 'cause I have to run to the bathroom now, I get so nervous. The one upstairs is safe, your man just sprayed again—and call me if you need me," and she goes waddling off with her clacking heels, pink housecoat—and the face of Native Dancer—as I take another deep breath and keep rubbing my fluttering eyelid!

"Herman, what'd you use?"

"Malathion, but I mixed it myself this morning! Look, Mr. Hagar, I sprayed ever damn *inch* of this house already and God knows I don't need nothin' else now with my son—"

"You told me—"

"—gettin' eighteen stitches in Youngstown, Ohio—"

"Herman, I know—"

"—him'n his cousin playin' with huntin' knives—"

"Herman?"

"—lucky he didn't take his freakin' arm off!"

"I know, Herman, I know, so why don't you take care of those things that're flitting around upstairs and I'll go have a look in the cellar, got some Diazinon in my bag."

"OK, OK, it's just, Mr. Hagar, I been under a helluva lotta pressure lately, kids'll drive ya crazy! Seems like they're always messin' themselves up when they get far away from home!"

"Yeah," and I go trotting down to the basement—Just what I need now, Herman with his slasher son! And thank God Boyne's still alive, can't believe him calling—shot at? wife's stealing his daughter? Comeback Show?—and how the hell can I go over, still haven't told my mother, made a reservation as my eyelid keeps twitching away—Christ, my nerves so damn *raw!* being pulled in three different directions: Boyne needing me there, my mother needing me here, and so needing Teri beside me!—flicking on these bright flourescents: this bare cellar running the length of the house with gray cinder block walls, a folded ping-pong table, and taking my flashlight and spray gun out of my bag to look behind this Sears hot water heater with these shaking, sweaty hands! Waterbugs usually follow the pipes straight up,

Herman probably giving them a fast spritz and missing most of that crawl space back there as I start blasting Diazinon all around—

And maybe I shouldn't go, just fly to North Dakota and try to patch up what's left of our marriage? Still feeling the press of Teri's goodbye!—ducking into this crawl space as I keep spraying side to side—but never giving up that dream of mine, and she screaming, "What it's been like *throughout* our marriage! You don't even realize for the last seven years all I've heard about is your Irish summer, Boyne and Ciara—you care more about your past or the characters you write about than real people you have to get involved with—unless they're perfect like Ciara!" "Ciara? Whatta you talking about?" "Your dream girl, perfect girl! Why don't you go back to her? You're still in love with her!" "'In love with her'? I haven't seen her in years. I can't even remember what she looks like." "O sure, that's why all I ever hear about is Ciara this and Ciara that: Why isn't my hair blonde, why aren't I as smart, as poetic, as sensitive as she was? Why don't you go back and find her? I'm sure you could steal her away!" "Teri, I never said—" "And the only time I ever see you come alive anymore is when you're talking about what I've *never* been a part of!"

And all so long ago: Ciara now married with kids of her own? Or dreaming of me in *her* turmoil? Living in the past, an eternal hazard, writing spurring it on—"You come home from that damn office and the termites and roaches and bedbugs hating the world and screaming at the slightest thing, because suddenly the only involvement you have is with your father's business that you've always hated and were terrified of taking over!"—Teri finally leaving and filing for divorce, the first divorce in my family! And Christ, so needing her now!—feel like I'm in a pressure cooker, end of my rope, about to explode!—and Boyne's desperate pleas! Last seen in front of the Irish pub, tears running down his bearded cheeks, beret tilted, back in Carnaween, really needing *me* now—or me really needing *him*? Seven years gone by—and back to Carnaween with all I'd ever wanted, all I'd ever dreamed? Flynn first telling me about him ("Born on a boat off the coast of Ireland but raised in

Valhalla, New York") on that stormy ship across and then again in Paris: a brilliantly gifted, Turner-like artist and underground legend, most promising painter of his generation — who became too controversial and far ahead of his time — and the work I saw was fantastic! Convincing me then to stay, he painting, me writing, and the hell with the exterminating business! "Christ, life is *leaping,* boy, never a lying down!" — O Jesus, I don't know! Recapture the past, a second chance to fulfill my dreams? So what the hell do I do? — backing quickly out of this crawl space with the sweat now pouring off me as I finish spraying all around, behind the water heater — and the phone shrilly ringing! — Mrs. Shish shouting from above, "Herman, would you get that, please?"

"Mr. Hagar?" Herman calling down from the cellar door. "It's for you, your mother's on the line'n I'm goin' outside, get a new spray can outta my truck."

" — OK, OK, fine," and picking up this wall phone below the stairs, "Yeah, Ma, what is it?" as my eyelid keeps twitching away!

"You're still out at the beauty's, huh, drivin' you crazy I'm sure. O just more trouble, you know, Rodriquez won't be back now till Tuesday, Mastro hadda go to the hospital, and you got calls in Bellmore, Patchogue — "

"*O dear GOD!!*" Mrs. Shish shrieking upstairs, "There's one in *MY* bathroom!"

" — and another somewhere in Hartsdale — "

"Get him *OUT* of here!!"

Blinking rapidly now, "Ma, how can I possibly go to Patchogue *and* Hartsdale?"

"O God, they're all *OVER* the place!!"

"Well then I would just do the ones in Bellmore and Patchogue — "

"I'm gonna have a *HEART ATTACK* right here in my *BATHROOM!!*"

Shouting, "Be right *up,* Mrs. Shish!" as I keep rubbing this goddamn eyelid!

"Gene, what's going on there?"

"Nobody ever *BELIEVES* me—"

"She's going banan—*CHRIST ALMIGHTY!!!*" and jumping a mile as a huge black waterbug goes crawling over my hand—and I swat it away—dropping the phone and stomping it dead—then hurling my spray gun across the room, noisily banging off the wall!!

("—Gene, Gene, are you *there?* What happened? What's going *on?* Are you *OK?*")

Snatching up the swaying receiver, "No, I'm *not* OK! I'm on the verge of a goddamn *breakdown* and if I don't get away from this business, the bugs and these customers, someone'll have to exterminate *me!!*"

"'Away'? Whatta you talking about 'away', not to Ireland and that *meshuggener?*"

"No, to London, Kew—"

"London? Whatta you saying? How can you possibly go to *London?"*

"I'll just get on a plane and go!"

"But there's the business and your wife just left—Gene, whatta you *crazy?*"

"Yeah, maybe I *am* crazy!"

"Will someone please get *UP* here!!"

"Now you wanna kill me too?"

"O Jesus, Ma!"

"—God, I'm gonna *DIE*, I'm gonna *DIE!!*"

"It wasn't enough with Ireland seven years ago when you almost killed your father?"

"I didn't *kill* my father and he didn't get sick 'cause I was in Ireland!"

Herman looking down, "Mr. Hagar, what's she screamin' about this time?"

"(Herman, just get the hell up there!) *THIS* stroke killed him, a real cerebral stroke!"

"All right already, what does it matter now, but how can you possibly go running off to London, three thousand miles away?"

"'Cause if I don't, I'm gonna have a fucking stroke of my *OWN!!*"

Boyne

Across the lush green meadows of Phoenix park with the blood leaping along my veins, past the Zoological Gardens—*Mary and Joseph!* the squeal of seals and the roar of those yawning lions (my nerves so on edge, picturing killers behind every hedge!)—and up to Sligo's elegant vine-covered domain, looking strangely seedy now, grayish paint peeling away, as I nip by the filigreed gate, skip onto the Doric porch, and begin rapping on this large gold knocker—nervously licking my lips, seafaring slicker rippling in the breeze (feeling so exposed and alone out here!)—as the black front door swings open with a creak and hoary old Ordway, deaf as a coot in his blue butler's suit, peers out with a doddering bow.

"Ah, *Ordway, dear* Ordway!" clasping his nodding head in my hands and kissing each of his bristled cheeks, "it's *marvelous* seeing you again!"

"—Is it *you*, s-sir?"

"It is *I*, Ordway, *only* I who's finally arrived here in the flesh! But how the hell've you *been?*"

"Thin, s-sir? Yes, well I may have lost some weight."

"But still looking rather *spry*, I'd say, for an old Sinn Féiner¯ like you!"

"Certainly, s-sir, right this way."

"And I'd just like to add how grieved I was to hear of your master's passing—trust that his daughters are to home?"

"No, you needn't have phoned. Any bags, s-sir?"

"No, no, Ordway, I shan't be staying, sorry—"

"In the car, s-sir? I'll go have a look round the car."

And sauntering past him with a grin down the long shadowed hall under these gilded portraits of Sligo's family, all dour-faced rhinos, and into this white-walled room: white carpets, white furniture (like being in a bloody asylum!)—and Good *God*, will you just *look* at that wondrous sight! One of my early works still blazing above the mantle: "Painting up a bloody *storm* then, Billy, with my worn brushes and palette knife, frenzied fingers and thumbnail gouging, scratching, and scrubbing cobalt green across a field of white—till gradually and, as if by magic, that widening gyre of color turned into lusty Laura nude in the throes of passion swathed in a Turner-like haze and seething vortex of light! O so young and supple-bellied she was in those days with her smooth buttermilk rump and breasts as plump as avocados!" **"Zounds, lad, but surely it was Renoir who said, 'A painter who has the feel of breasts and buttocks is truly saved'!"** "Right, and now here she is stealing my *girl!*" as I keep pacing around in my growing state of agitation, circling this white-carpeted floor, "Last time I was back in Baltimore, whisking Tory away to the Museum of Art, hiding out till they were closed, then slowly emerging to see it the only way you should, by flashlight and alone! Some people spend a lifetime studying those paintings, Billy, but we needed only a night—and Laura calling the police, swore she'd kill me if I ever came near her again—and I had to flee back to Ireland once more! Such a selfish bloody *bitch* she's become, avenging *whore*—"

And the door flying open with a thunderous slam as Sligo's two spinsterish daughters come prancing in, "O Mr. Boyne, we've been so trying to *find* you!"

"Brenda, please!" older sister, Vi, brandishing a vinyl riding crop, now striding on by with those tan hairy tweeds and ball-bearing eyes as the frilly, flirting Brenda flitters behind, sheathed in white organdy and ruffles of lace and twining her long feather boa.

"Find me—why?"

"O nothing, nothing at all, Mr. Boyne, Brenda was just so delighted to see you." Brenda still flirting and giggling with glee. "But please do sit down, and would you care for a drink, an apéritif or there's red wine, white wine?"

"O any wine'll do!" Brenda drifting sinuously toward the sideboard. "Though I must say when I learned of your father's passing, lost myself for a month or more in the bogs of incognito—Ah, that's very kind, could really use one now!" draining this crystal glass in a gulp, "—But what in God's name happened?"

"Well we're none of us quite certain, the weight of his years, a final straw, I doubt we shall ever know."

"So it had nothing to do with my show?"

"Your show? O dear Lord no, not at all, not in the slightest, Mr. Boyne! In fact, we *have* been trying to find you—"

Brenda behind me now, "And you'll never know how consoling during this period your paintings truly were," tracing her feather boa seductively across my nape, "Found them terribly, *terribly* exciting—" over my ears—

"Brenda?" under my nose—

"—they just opened me up completely—"

"Brenda, please!"

"And you *look* so wonderful!"

Thwack! Vi's riding crop whacking her thigh as I shoot straight up out of my chair!

"Smell so wonderful—"

"Yes, well Mr. Boyne," Vi pausing in profile before the mantle with her long-lipped rhino face as Brenda and her boa continue twining toward backpedaling me, "you must be looking forward to your show tomorrow night?"

"O far *more* than that, ladies," dodging deftly round this ottoman, "since I came to what can only be called an extraordinary decision this morning talking to Turner—"

"Turner, Mr. Boyne?"

" — concerning the Tate!" weaving between white settees —

"O I adore Turner, simply adore —"

"Brenda, please — So you've been in *contact* with the Tate?"

"No not at all —"

"O Vi and I were just there for a board —"

"Yes, yes, well what Brenda's referring to is the fact of our recently succeeding our father as trustees for life, Mr. Boyne —"

"Trustees for *life*, ha-ha!" as I feint right and zip left round the sofa, " 'Cause suddenly out there on those tracks, Billy told me —"

Thwack! "Brenda, please!"

" — if I can just get one of my works hung in the Tate, my struggles will all be worth it!"

"Yes, of course, Mr. Boyne, but we still haven't received the remainder of your works for *this* show."

"O just some last-minute touching up to do, Vi, be bringing them over myself, you know."

"Ah, that's grand, because we *are* counting on you," Vi rapidly tapping the riding crop in her hand as Brenda now comes gliding in from behind, *ha-ha!* "and as far as the Tate goes, you have my word —" *thwack!* " — we'll provide you whatever support we can."

"Ah, that's marvelous, bloody *marvelous*, Vi, you're an angel in disguise!" being forced into this corner — and Ordway comes doddering in —

". . . Still haven't found your bags yet, s-sir —" as I sidestep her once again.

"Yes, Ordway, well that'll be all."

"Of course, m-madam," and he goes bowing and doddering out as Brenda continues chasing me about — thinks she's performing a Noel Coward play — snaking that sensuous boa across my beret!

"O this is all so exciting, I can hardly *wait* for your show!" with Vi now sliding between us as I go veering toward the door.

"Yes, well we're *both* looking forward to it, Mr. Boyne, and all we ask is that you give us your word — Brenda, will you please *stop!* — that by tomorrow night everything will be complete?"

"O absolutely, ladies —" reaching the hall, "— you have my fervent vow that tomorrow night in Londontown you'll see The Comeback Show of the *Century!*"

Hagar

Coming down through this late morning mist over the immense sprawled shimmer of the Irish Sea, a green, toppling sea, dots and white smears of sailboats and the sunny hill of what must be Howth, wild flowers blooming, those heathery, hedgerowed fields, Pigeon House and Poolbeg Flasher, palms sweating, my free hand sliding back and forth over the blue musty edge of my raincoat hem — another plane out there, silver glint fading in the distance — and I *still* can't believe I'm on my way to London, leaving that goddamn business behind, Mrs. Shish's waterbugs, accountants coming in Tuesday, and my mother's final pleas, "Crazy altogether! You couldn't take a day or two out in the Hamptons, we could go together, why all of a sudden *London?*"

One of these sexy stewardesses passing by, the smooth-fitting green tweed of her airline suit snugly accentuating her swaying rump as she moves down the aisle, offering assorted sweets and masking the small fire of annoyance that flickers within — Last chance, said Boyne, before I'm engulfed *forever* in the bug business — he needing me — but so needing *him* now with everything in my life exploding, marriage falling apart — speeding on, my dreams of escape, flying through flung nets out of reach, heading back to the world of my past. . . .

31

To Carnaween in that summer of 1960: our mad, whirl-wind spree, Boyne's twelve-room house by the Irish Sea—and now seven years later at thirty-eight, God knows what he's like, the incredible Seamus Boyne, trying to take his life—or someone doing it for him? Should've called him before, told him my flight—maybe thinks I'm not coming, can't wait any longer, slitting his wrists, blowing his brains out—*No*, stop it, stop it, sure he's OK, *must* be OK!

And in those seven years since we met what have I become: a man enchanted with the world (Teri saying, "You were that way when we met!") or just jumping out of my skin, locked in my father's office and letting no one in? Not what I was then—thirty-one now, nose with its Roman bump and the shock of high-school hair fast receding, my father's widow's peak—accepted then as Joyce's forehead, my monumental conceit, seeking someone to back my dreams, spin illusions, and let me fly. And my father screaming the day that I left, his raccoon eyes squinting in the sun, "The biggest mistake we made was sending you to Columbia, one graduate school was enough. You've gotta settle down, start earning a living like the rest of your friends. This was your last semester, I'm not paying for any more schools, Cornell, Yale, now Columbia—*enough* already! After this trip you come into business!"

A final fling, his summer bonus, before I settled down. And going, not knowing what to do, running I knew not where—till I ran into Ciara that first night in Paris, a dazzling blonde Swedish-looking girl with bluestone eyes and dimpled cheeks, who loved Joyce, Dylan, and Synge, spoke five languages fluently, the brightest girl I've ever met, up at the Contrescarpe to see Flynn perform (Boyne's art school pal, "Part-time Actor, Painter, Balladeer: A Superior Catholic Standing at Stud") as I just kept staring at her and finally worked up my nerve to ask, "But you're not *Irish*, are you?" "Pardon?" and she smiled as I kept on staring, her eyes roaming over my face. "I said, you're not Irish—?" "I am Irish? No, not entirely." "Then you must be Swedish." "No, I must be Dutch." "Dutch? Yes, well I think you're very pretty and I hope you understood what I just said."

And Flynn still singing as she smiled again, "But *you* are not Irish, are you?" "No, just American, bewildered American." "Ah, and I was nearly thinking you were Irish. But what do you do? You are a singer also?" "No, I write." "I see. Is that your ambition, or are you already fulfilled?" "How old are you?" "You want to know how *old* I am? Nineteen, but very soon I shall be twenty." "Very soon. By the way, my name is Gene." "Gene, and I am Keer-ah." "Keer-ah?" "Yes, it is spelled with a C, C-i-a-r-a. An uncle of mine was Irish, though my family actually is from Delft." "Dutch-Irish? I never heard of that." Flynn kneeling down from the stage above, his orange curls and mustache reeling, "Never *heard* of it, Gene? Jaysus, if the Dutch had Ireland it'd be a garden and if the Irish had Holland, they'd all drown!" as her English boyfriend suddenly appeared in his deerstalker cap and pinstriped slacks and off we sped to their houseboat on the Seine, Ciara, Milo, Flynn, and I.

(And God, she's *still* so vivid to me, her ability to make it all seem possible, be anything I wanted her to be!)

Then next morning, after we'd stayed up to bring in the dawn with Flynn staggering away to Belleville and Milo to British Intelligence, Ciara and I went capering all around the Louvre and down to the Grecian rooms, she peeking in and out of those marble statues or gracefully posing with her hand upheld.

"Ciara, listen, did you ever play tag in Holland?"

"Of course, only we didn't call it that. Why, you don't want to play *here*, do you?"

"Why not? I'll bet I can catch you—and you're it!"

"But the guards?"

"Asleep in the Egyptian rooms. I'll count to ten, give you a head start, so you'd better get going. One—"

"Wait! Let me take off these then," doffing her high heels, "At least you can make it fair, with you wearing your gym, your tennis shoes, and I'll put mine here," placing her purse in a corner, "I could not run very fast, elude you, carrying them, could I now?"

"Two. No, you couldn't. Three. Better get going. Four—"

And she was off, past pediments and pedestals, Etruscan amphorae and a tulip-shaped vase, noble busts and limbless torsos to disappear giggling round a Caesar head, Octavian pose, as the tourists smiled, frowned, stepped aside, my sneakered feet darting this way, that, not far behind her hair of Scandinavian shine, harried glance over her shoulder as she dizzily turned a corner on one foot—and by God, she was gone! Passing votive sculptures, Venus, the caryatids, and back to the Greeks for a fast look in—and there she was, barefoot under a bronze Apollo, poised, panting, waiting to move, didn't see me, couldn't hear me, creep up behind—"*Eeeee!!*"

"*Got* you!" whirling her round and round.

"O *God*, Gene!" collapsing back against me, "I never even heard you!" as I nuzzled her small cup of bone where the collar came away, and she kept gazing up at the statue, "And who is that?"

"Apollo."

Ciara whispering in my ear, "He has your Roman nose."

"Only the nose?"

She laughing, "Though he does have a rather small penis, doesn't he?"

"Probably just finished showering."

"But that doesn't happen to you too, all shriveled up?"

"Don't you know?"

"Not things like this. Shy little me with my Calvinistic—"

"I know, nineteen and never been kissed, ho ho!"

And following the arrows to the dark polished floors of the Grande Galerie as she shook loose her hair with a bright flashing smile (her front teeth's slight charming overlap), the blonde down shimmering on her arms and the sweat of health glimmering on her brow, lithe hips swaying in her prideful gait, the ripe swell of her breasts straining against the balance and poise of her motion, animal balance and poise and that spark of impulsive gaiety, her tight-fitting blue skirt snugly accentuating her sassy rump, firm outline of her panties, dark elliptical folds of her blouse. "Ciara, I love to see what your body does to clothes, swelling and curving them into a sensual shape! *Je t'aime, ma*

chérie, Liebe also, and how do you say love in Dutch?" *"Liefde. Ik
ben gek op jou als ik bij je ben."*

And cramming all my delights, insights, and insistent need
into that whirlwind week or more as Milo left for Liechtenstein
and I kept galloping down to their houseboat on the Seine. And
what did I really offer? Words, dreams, create the conscience of
my race, pen *Ulysses* ten years after? Writer, wife, come share my
hazardous life, or common-law lovers like Joyce and Nora—
Milo returning, the two of us vying for her, and Ciara couldn't
decide, "Gene, I don't really know if I could even live your
dream, but I promise I will write if I should change my mind."

And a few days later I left for Ireland alone, hoping her letter
would be waiting, posted on to Dublin and reposing under the
dust. Didn't really expect it. Hoped, to be sure, though not much
more.

But her letter *was* waiting at the American Express:

> Dear Gene,
> If Ireland is half as lovely as you told me, please
> write me, and I will come.

"Christ *Almighty!!!*"
Heads turning and staring at my whoop of joy, "Sorry,
sorry," as I went skipping the light fantastic out the door, give me
that old soft shoe, I said that old soft shoe, ah one, ah two, ah
clickety-clackety boo! The Irish leaning back, wide-eyed,
eschewing me—Screw!—for there was champagne in my
sneakered feet, Mumm's bubbly, all my senses with their hands
in their pockets as I gamboled down toward the heart of the city,
raincoat tossed carelessly over my shoulder, in my wine-colored
T-shirt, khakis, and white Converse All-Stars—under the
stained gray shade of the Bank of Ireland, pigeons balanced along
the narrow ledge, and stepping suddenly into a bright patch of
sunlight, my shadow flung out before me, through Bewley's
Oriental aroma and down Westmoreland Street at half-past the
hour by the *Irish Times* with church bells ringing and my
reflection in the shop windows flickering near, a wild and rowdy

brown bear singed by the summer, unruly shock of hair, the girls with rosepink smears on their cheeks, and sea gulls zealously flapping like torn white wrapping paper in the breeze as I followed the green double-decker buses on toward the river, the Liffey slowly flowing along with oil slicks and refuse wallowing about its shaggy banks.

O I had it *all*, Ireland, Joyce, and Ciara on her way, Boyne convincing me to stay, he painting, me writing, reading aloud to him every night or admiring his amazing talent, days of rain and grass, trees and paths, sketching in the canoe, all I'd ever wanted, all I'd ever dreamed as we jigged together in Carnaween — till that telegram from my mother arrived:

Dad suffered a stroke. You must come home.

And that last grey morning with Boyne in great agitation (and looking like a wild-eyed Augustus John) walking me down to the bus and waiting outside the pub in the blustery rain, wearing his beret, sunglasses, and that billowing green windbreaker.

"Good *God*, Gene, just why the hell're you *going?* I mean what the hell for? Listen to me, will you, and take my word — I know all about American mothers'n their ways, he's probably OK — 'cause you're making the biggest mistake of your *life* leaving here!"

"Seamus, I have to go back and see how he is!"

"Just *stay* here, will you! America's mad, insane! Ireland's the *only* place to paint, to write and do one's art — I mean you leave now and you'll *never* come back! Suffering *Christ*, end up a bug man living in Great Neck! I mean we've got it all here, Gene, everything you wanted. You *yourself* said so and you're a writer, hell of a writer, really, all the elements're there, I heard your work and the way you handle language and, Jesus, you *have* to write, this dream girl's coming over — so Christ, you can't leave *now!*"

"Seamus, I'll be back and I wrote Ciara to wait —"

"Good *God*, boy, at least call your mother first — just to check if it's true — but you don't *leave*, there's no reason to leave, just toss it all away! God*damn* it, Gene, you *have* to stay, started painting again *'cause* of you, never painted *better*, period of my greatest creativity—"

"Seamus, I give you my word—"

"Making the biggest *mistake*—" The bus splashing and swaying round the bend, "—biggest mistake of your *life*—"

"Probably be back in another week."

"—I'm telling you, you'll be *sorry*—Listen to me, Gene, I know!"

Shaking his hand, "Goodbye, Seamus," and hugging him, "be back before you know it."

"—Biggest mistake of your *life* leaving here!!"

Still muttering to himself within the shelter of the doorway as I mounted the bus, a wave over my shoulder and down the aisle toward an empty seat, my luggage dropped on the floor. And turning around as we slowly pulled away, I glanced back to see him huddled in the doorway, the tears running under his sunglasses and down his bearded cheeks—

"Ladies and gentlemen, we are beginning our descent into London now. Fasten your seatbelts, please."

*   *   *

Along this rainy towpath, rushes and poplar trees churning above the Thames and that rising tide of anxiety sweeping over me again—arriving too late and Boyne's already dead!—Jesus, where the hell's his *home?* Never gonna find it! This the way to go? Past a pale brick row of Edwardian cottages, jets coming in low through those storm clouds overhead, this windy drizzle flapping and slapping my blue raincoat all about me, drenching my small valise—and the leafy path sharply curving round to this secluded little cottage down by the river—must be Tattersall Wharf!—most of the lawn's been cut, flowerpots along the window sills as I hurry on toward this flaking green door—

And a thunderous peal of organ music bellowing out, dark keening chords—*Holy Christ*, Boyne (or who knows) in there writhing over the keys, about to do himself in!

Pounding on the knocker again and again, then shouting, "*Seamus?*" The music resounding through the windy air. "Seamus, it's me, Gene, I'm *here!* I'm *here!*" banging on these latticed panes, still can't see who it is, riddled and tinselly with rain—and the organ suddenly stopping, echoes wheezing away—

"Ah *Hagar*, ha-ha! Be with you in just a jiff!"

And the door flying open with bearded Boyne standing there stark naked—except for his beret and those green-striped socks—grinning from ear to ear, "Good *God*, boy, right in the middle of my *concerto*, ha-ha!"

"Seamus, are you *OK*, weren't about to—?"

"OK?" laughing, "Jesus!" the whites of his eyes glazed with a fiery myopic glare.

"—I mean—What the hell're you, *drunk?*"

"*Drunk?* Why of course I'm *drunk!* Wasn't Bach drunk? Turner drunk? Fucking Brian Boru? And it's bloody *marvelous* seeing you, Gene!" shaking my hand with both of his, "But come in, come in—O Christ, I don't have any *clothes* on hea-ah! Appear to have forgotten my entire *ensemble*, ha-ha, and you in your Ivy finery thea-ah," leaning forward and looking out from side to side, "Anybody else with you?"

"No."

"You sure?"

"Yes. Why?"

"Thought I heard other footsteps."

"No, just mine."

"Fine, fine, just being careful, you know, all sorts of creatures lurking about, regularly occurring incidents—"

"Why, what else happened?"

"—I'll just whip on some togs and be down in a flash!"

And he goes loping up the stairs, his lean, rangy body, bouncing balls, and fleshy white ass streaked with a bright greenish smear as I take another deep breath in this hall before a row of dazzling Turner-like paintings of shadowy couples making love in all sorts of positions bathed in a shimmering, swirling light. *Fantastic* they are! Even better than the last ones I saw—all this work he's done over the years while I've let the years drift by!—and turn right into a room literally *filled* with Guinness bottles, hundreds of them glistening in silhouette, tumbles of books, boxes, and an old-fashioned organ (like the one in Ireland: the two of us dancing a madcap jig, laughing uncontrollably) as Boyne comes cantering down wearing a frayed red sweatshirt with the hood bouncing behind and a pair of gray seersucker shorts.

"Ah Gene, found the Guinness Room yourself, have you, navigating round me bottles?"

"Jesus Christ, how many *are* there?"

"O three or four thousand—but they're all *over* the bloody house!—been commuting back and forth incognito, cornering the Guinness market in Delgany and now half of Kew, ha-ha!" his sinister throaty laugh exposing his whitish teeth—a thin gap along the bottom row—within his grizzled beard.

"But I thought you were into wine."

"Well I am! Just a variation of Gandhi's line: I believe in God so long as he takes the shape of a bottle, ha-ha! And Hagar, you really *got* here, didn't you?" slapping my arm and broadly grinning, "It's absolutely *marvelous* seeing you again—"

"Yeah, it's great seeing you—"

"—alive and kicking, and ready for my Comeback Show, 'Your Show of Shows'—The Comeback Show of the *Century!*" and chortling, he goes loping by the organ, raking his shaggy beard, "Though Jesus, you caught me by surprise, so damn hectic now, working nonstop, then flying over last night—just wasn't sure when you'd arrive!" quickly lighting up a Player's from a pack in his pocket and flipping the match over his shoulder, "But tell me, Gene, how the blazes *you* are! You look the same with that mop of floppy hair, the All-American boy with his Apollonian flair! And marriage seems to've aged you, like vintage wine, *Irish* wine—Well hell, it's *been* seven years, we had a few laughs, had a few tears—and now you've fled your home, wife's left so you could roam! Well how does it *feel* off on this spree—?"

"God only knows," tripping over these bottles—

"—up to your ears in bugs—"

"—what's going on with my life!" this damn eyelid twitching again!

"—and now *King* of the Bloody Bugs! Well everybody's going buggy these days anyway, ha-ha! But Suffering Christ, how does it feel to take over the Vermin Empire, become a Captain of *Pest* Control?"

"It's driving me out of my mind!" striding by the latticed windows, "No, I'm serious, Seamus, everything in my life's exploding, I just had to get away! I mean, you know, this time my father really has a stroke and dies and now here I am *running* it, my wife taking—"

"Wait, what do you mean 'really' has a stroke? You received that telegram from your mother when you were over—"

"I know, but you were right, that was just to get me back, he was simply exhausted, needed rest, and was out of the hospital before I got home. Anyway, the point is now I am running the business, what I've hated all these years, driving me up the wall—"

"Or one day awake as a Franz Kafka cockroach waiting to be stomped on, ha-ha!"

"—never really involved—"

"Remember that marvelous line Franz said to *his* father, Gene: 'Think of me as a dream'?"

"—just drifting along and now locked in my father's office!"

"Yes, but now we're *together* again! And you can't tell me all these years all you've been doing is stomping out *roaches*? Jesus, boy, you need training for that, lessons with José Greco to master the art of the flamenco," and clapping his hands and snapping his head, he stamps out his half-smoked Player's, "*Olé!*"

"No, but seriously, Seamus—" as I keep rubbing this fluttering eyelid— "so much's been going on in my life with my father, the business, marriage falling apart, that I really needed to *talk* to you now!"

"O I know, I know, can feel what you're going through, believe me I do, and it'll all work itself out, I promise you—But first let me tell you about my show—have you seen the *Times?*"

reaching atop the organ, "the *London Times?* Ad here, half a *page* practically!" pointing to a large box in the left-hand corner:

Now the long-awaited Comeback of the
Most Controversial Painter of his Generation:
SEAMUS EAMON BOYNE
The Sligo-Moeran Gallery
62 Cadogan Square

"Isn't that bloody *marvelous*, ha-ha!" lighting up another Player's and tossing the match over his shoulder, "All part of our strategy, Gene, all part of our dreams!"

"Yeah, some dreams!" and pacing again, "For seven years all *I've* been doing is working in the shadow of my father, now he dies, my mother's driving me *crazy*—"

"Gene, later, later, we'll sort it later—"

"—then my wife takes off—"

"—never let you down before and have no intention of doing so now—"

"—my marriage suddenly over—"

"—but Good *God*, Hagar, more than anyone, I know what it's like to end a marriage, lose a daughter."

"—Yeah, well what's that all about?"

Boyne adjusting his beret and snuffing out another half-smoked Player's, "O they won't let me see her, see my only girl, burnished little girl, but I do, *still* do, they can't stop me, *never* stop me—" the whites of his eyes growing glossy, "—no one is taking my *girl!*" as sniffling, he turns the other way, raking his grizzled beard, "O I'll *see* her all right! Damn right I'll see her! Be back in Baltimore, what is it, next week for the hearing and when she sees what her father's become—not what they've told her—my talent finally recognized, she'll come back to Carnaween!"

"You're going over next *week?*"

"Well, you know, just to clear this up, in and out in a jiff— But Gene, come on with me for a minute," as he goes loping into the hall, " 'cause there's something I want you to see!"

And really feeling uneasy here, things somehow not the same — but so needing to talk to him now with my eyelid still twitching away — as I enter this wide skylighted room with its tall black walls, an easel standing in the center, his multicolored palette, cans of oily water, brushes sprouting from earthenware pots, open tubes of paint, and Boyne, like P. T. Barnum with a flourishing sweep of his hand, presenting it all to me:

"Pure, sunless light from the north, Gene, pure as light can be!"

"Yeah, well I've been married now for seven years —"

"Light *bursting* out of darkness!"

" — soon after I got home —"

And still grinning like a horse with his lips curling away from his teeth, he steps back from his canvas of a beautiful blonde-haired girl amid a radiant swirl of color seductively offering herself from the rear —

"*Holy Christ!* but that's — that's *CIARA!*" The same bright flashing smile —

"Isn't she *marvelous?*"

— slight charming overlap, tiptilted nose. "But where, how the hell'd you *meet* her?" whirling quickly around, "Is she *here?*"

"No, she's there before you on canvas, recreated from your words!"

"My *words?* But how'd you ever — ?"

"When you read me your work seven years ago, it was those descriptions of her I remembered after you'd left and I couldn't afford real models that ignited these blazing visions —"

"But why *that* pose?"

"Soul of a bearded Celtic satyr, ha-ha!"

"But all I did was *describe* her —"

"And I took it from there!"

"How many more — ?"

"O portraits galore, which've never been seen till now! But you really think I've captured her?"

"It's incredible! But come on, tell me the truth, where the hell'd you meet her?"

"Believe me, Gene, it's only your words, I swear!"

"And all these years you've been—"

"Producing the finest works of my career—though you'd never know it from my reviews and that host of disastrous shows before I started painting Ciara!" picking up his palette with his right hand and a long dark brush in his left, "'Cause making love and painting've always been one and the same to me, same expenditure of energy, same virile joy—"

"Yeah, I can see, I can see, but—"

"—and the sensate tip of my brush," Boyne leaning forward now and sideways to his right, "is like an organ of physical pleasure, an inseparable part of me—" laying on the paint with a kind of brute relish—

"Yeah, well it's still a helluva shock to me!"

"—the surface of my canvas like living skin," applying sensuous strokes of red and green, "but listen, all I'm really doing, Gene, is making public what Turner did in private—"

"—*everything* getting crazy now—"

"—those lusty sketches of naked lovers that Ruskin burned in a fit of Victorian pique!"

Jesus *Christ*, he doesn't even *HEAR* me!! This whole trip becoming a nightmare—you can't repeat the past!—and that rising tide of anxiety rushing over me again, rubbing this goddamn eyelid!—as he keeps on painting, using the palm of his hand to blend all those tints together—

"Heighten these round persimmon nipples and pubic hair like wild mountain thyme! And soon, Hagar, she'll be hanging in the Tate beside Turner—"

God, I can hardly *breathe!!* as I go racing blindly out of his studio, down this hall and tripping, stumbling through the door—still drizzling, the wind scudding the falling leaves along this towpath with the Thames below tossing about—*had* to get out of there, couldn't talk to him, make it clear, feeling so out of place, sight of Ciara, offering herself from the rear—just breathe, keep on breathing—has his *own* problems here, Comeback Show, losing his daughter, and now I appear, needing to talk about *me!*

Down this lane behind the Edwardian cottages and out onto Bushwood Road toward that black cab waiting—

"Hagar, Good *God!!*" Boyne grabbing me from behind as I hop into this taxi, "where the hell are you *going?*" and he hops in too and slams the door.

"—I-I don't know!"

"Where to, sir?"

"I looked around and suddenly felt like I did, Mother of Christ, when my daughter was *taken* from me! Just drive, keep driving!"

"But where, sir?"

"Around the fountain and take it slow!"

And off we go with a rasp of gears round that small stone fountain out there.

"But Gene, what's the matter, why on earth'd you *leave?*"

"'cause I couldn't talk to you, felt—I don't know—Seamus, look, it's not your fault—I just thought it'd be like Ireland again, but you can't repeat the past, turn back the clock."

"Turn back the clock, no, but you sure as hell can rewind it!"

"Now where, sir?"

"Damn it, man, just keep driving till I tell you to stop!"

"But where to, sir?"

"Around the fountain!"

"*Again*, sir?"

"Yes, again and *again!* But Good *God*, Gene, you're here and that's all that matters now!" as we putter around the fountain once more, "The two of us together and back to Carnaween! 'Cause I still have the house, the castle—and I've always believed in you and your writing, unlike your father—"

"I know but—"

"—and especially now when you're being sucked down into that business you've always hated—'cause seven years ago, hell, I was where you are now with a wife just having left and you got me painting again—Driver, driver, go the *other* way now, I'm getting dizzy with just one direction!—and I know the kind of free spirit, Gene, you really are, what all of them back there probably've never *seen*! 'Cause all they know back there is Hagar the *bugman* or Hagar the *homeowner* or Hagar the *consumer*— haven't got a clue as to what's going on *inside* you!"

"Seamus—"

"No, no, *listen*, just imagine someone like Beethoven back there buying chopmeat in one of those Muzaked supermarkets while the Fifth Symphony is going off inside his head: 'One pound of ground round, please.' *Dada da Dum!* 'That'll be sixty-nine cents a pound, sir.' *Da-da da DUM!* O Suffering *Christ*, what a scene! All those suburban matrons fighting behind him, trying to bump him out of line, the bloody Muzak going—and all they know is that little old deaf man who buys chopmeat and reads lips! Enough, driver, our circular journey's over, we're getting out right hea-ah! What's our fare?"

"One pound, sir, should cover it."

"Right, and keep the change. Most refreshing spin, must do this again some time!" and back along the leafy towpath with his arm around my shoulder, "And now you know *why* you're coming, Gene, not like before, running from your father, vaguely seeking Joyce," under these shimmering willows, "know bloody well where you *are*!"

"Yeah, on the verge of a nervous—"

"'Cause the art is *always* worth it and you *need* an immediate change, the freedom and distance to do your work!" Speedboats bouncing over the gray and choppy Thames. "And as for females, we've an *abundance* of 'em, one of our Irish beauties, exquisitely slim colleens—O the country is just full of 'em waiting to serve, concubines galore! And now your wife has opened the door, so as soon as I succeed, of course we'll leave and you'll come back to Carnaween!" side by side up the flagstone path with his arm still round my shoulder.

"Yeah, well God knows, Seamus, if I'm ready for Ireland now, 'cause lately everything's driving me crazy!"

"Ah, then you'd better come out back now, shoot some baskets and restore your sanity!"

"Baskets?" following him through the door, "But it's still raining—"

"No, no, those are just windswept clouds, sun'll soon be blazing!" and back into the Guinness Room as he kicks some bottles aside, "Come on, boy, once you restore your sanity and put things in perspective, none of them can ever *touch* you, 'cause you do seem a little tense."

"Me, *tense?* How could you possibly tell? And since when are you playing basketball?"

"Ah, well see, Dungannon put it up, became a rather fanatic Celtic fan — but let me just find the ball," and he goes searching through the room in his beret, red-hooded sweatshirt, and seersucker shorts, kicking aside the drapes — "Ah, here we *are!*" holding up a dusty Spalding and wiping it off, "Knew it was around here somewhere, picked it up at Harrods where they've everything, elephant tusks and Assam tea — but listen, Gene, you know you could take off that raincoat now 'cause it hardly ever rains in here — *and* your jacket and tie, and I'll go get some sneakers, an extra pair in my room," and loping rapidly up the stairs, he goes rummaging around up there, the sound of clinking bottles, then comes cantering down again, "Adidas blue and whites — those all right?"

"Fine, just what I need right now," shaking my head and lacing them up, "a game of basketball!"

"But you *played* basketball, didn't you, within those hallowed Ivy walls of Cornell and Yale? Good God, an Ivy League *Jew* — Amazing! The Irish'd have you running for Lord Mayor if they only knew! You could win in a *breeze* — Or no, it was soccer that you played, now I remember. Though actually you do look like a soccer player, thick neck, brawny. What position?"

"Fullback."

"Fullback, yes, blocking them off from the goal. Well I used to run track myself, a sprint man, real quick, ha-ha!" and back out the front door he goes with the wind still blustery and shafts of sunlight suddenly slanting between the clouds, "See, just look at the *weather* you brought! Absolutely *marvelous*, Hagar!" his loping stride and his red hood flapping behind, "O this weather is *unbelievable*, makes me feel like Ireland for once! Really, this is the first time it's felt like Ireland since I arrived — except there are no people there, just pigs, cattle, and an odd assortment of elves—Well hell, like when *you* were there—on the ground, in the green, near a glade!" around the side to a damp blacktopped drive and a white fan-shaped backboard, rusty orange rim, nailed over the garage, a window above it, "But here, let me try, see if I can make a quick ten in a row! Actually the first time I've been out, Gene, haven't done this in *years!*" flipping the ball left-handed toward the hoop with an excessive amount of spin—he finally banks one in, "Ah, think I've found the range . . . No—" as the next shot rims the basket and rolls off, "—not quite yet. Here, Gene, you try for a while," tossing the wet ball toward me with a casual flick of his wrist—that misses me by a yard, "—Sorry there, I can get it—"

"No, no, I've got it," bouncing it off the damp ground and up with a soft fadeaway jump—swish. Putting in several short jumpers in a row, then a long floating hook.

"Christ, you don't *miss*, Hagar!"

"Yeah, well I've been practicing," another fadeaway jump from the corner, "Have my own basket at home—"

"O you do, do you, out there every night, eh?"

"—Just about."

"How many in a row is that?"

"I don't know—six, seven."

"Right, well here, let me show you my Helen Keller shot, Gene, high percentage shot, never fails, usually do it with a blindfold," dribbling back, two fast bounces, then eyes closed, he steps forward and heaves the ball—*crashing* through the upstairs window! "O Good *God!*" shattered glass tinkling down, "Bit off course there—" as I burst out laughing, can't *stop* laughing—now both of us laughing—as he bumps into me, doubled up and roaring uncontrollably like we used to long ago, his arm around my shoulder, "—And—O Suffering *Christ!*—to think, Gene—" Boyne adjusting his beret as he gains a giggling breath, "—I once led the Art School League in scoring! Though that's not saying very much—with all those fruitcakes prancing about, you were more likely to get fondled rather than fouled, ha-ha!"

"—Yeah," and still smiling and drying my eyes with the back of my hand, "I think we'd better clean this up."

"O right y'are, whiskbroom's just here in the garage, have the glaziers pop out tomorrow," and sweeping the glass into my dustpan, "But listen, that's enough sport for today," dumping it into a trashbin, "'cause you'll never convince *me* you flew three thousand miles, left your wife, just to play basketball here in Kew!" and back around the house once more with our arms about each other, "For there's wine and women and wonders *galore* before we reach Jerusalem—and a party at my show besides!"

"What party's this?"

"Behind the gallery in Cadogan Square," passing these uncut hedges, "though we won't get there till late anyway, keep 'em *panting* for my arrival—then off to Ireland where there's still poetry and the dance! The dance, you see, is what's gone out of America, the old romance—and now, Gene, we'll be bringing it *back* to Ireland!"

"Organ and all?"

"O of course, 'cause I do know three notes: fee, fi, and fo."

"No fum?"

"Never had time for fum, ha-ha!" and through the flaking green door, "Come on, I'll play you the dance right now!"

"But what time's your show?"

"O I don't know, eight, eight-fifteen? *Irish* time—no such thing as eight precisely—give or take a millennium or two!" his loping stride, beret, and a thick curl of hair at his neck, swinging back into the Guinness Room—with seemingly even more bottles than before, bottles all over the place: on tables, chairs, in corners, throughout the dusty bookshelves, on top of the organ, within a grate, on settees, love seats, and this worn floral rug as he kicks some out of the way, pulling up a swivel stool, and adjusting his black beret in a mirror on the wall, "Now a bit of the trill to begin!" pumping the pedals, a loud diapason welling out, "Touch of the E. Powers Biggs—Ah Gene, what a marvelous hour for music, feeling at one with the few remaining *four*-footed creatures out there! Well Good *God*, I finally knew that here in this garden of Kew I, too, was one of nature's endangered species, along with the pig-footed bandicoot, the West African manatee, and the Block Island meadow vole, ha-ha!" Boyne grinning and rearing back and forth over the deep, wheezing chords as he keeps on warming up, "But hea-ah, a little Bach for Squire Hagar now from Great Neck! Though actually this is a Prelude and Fugue fusing with a Toccata and Passacaglia—O Christ, what a cadenza, pedal trill!—'cause Bach lost nine sons himself, went blind—his eyesight returning ten days before his death—but *still* drove on till the very end," a tender smile upon his lips, swaying from side to side, "and proved it was all worth it!" as he abruptly breaks it off, "Ah, but *enough* of that now, far too sad—How about an Irish reel or 'The Wild Rover'?" glancing up, the whites of his eyes gleaming with delight, grinning teeth, gap-tooth and all, beard and beret as he writhes over the keyboard, gay with the lilt of this Irish reel, leaning back, left foot pounding to keep up the rhythm and the music pealing madly away, "It *gets* you, doesn't it, boy? Come on, Gene, *into* it now! Show me some steps, a bit of the jig like we used to do—*fling* yourself into it! To Hagar's cutting the cord, an *Umbilical* Reel, it's time for a *CELEBRATION!!!*"

The lively beat thundering on and into it I go, heel and toe, slowly at first, dancing in place—God, haven't done this since Ireland! as he quickens the pace—hands on hips and crossing over, feet flicking, kicking out, "Ah *Jesus*, that's it! Clog dance, boy, goat dance, *Bumpa, bumpa, bumpa!*" mind zigzagging as I whirl about, gathering momentum, heels flung out—and Boyne leaving a long lingering note as I begin to slow, "Wait, don't fade now, we'll give 'em a show!" and head high lifted, knees well lifted, hands down, stiff at his sides, and singing, "*Bumpa, bumpa, bumpa!*" off he goes, do-si-do, linking arms and whirling right, linking arms and whirling left, my thighs aching, his red hood flapping, "*Bumpa-bumpa-bumpa!*" to sashay forward and sashay back—faster and faster and round once more, panting, kicking, my feet still flicking, mind a blur, a whirling daze—'till we spin to a dizzying stop and topple backward into these chairs!

Irish Wine

" — O *Christ*, that's enough leaping for a *lifetime*, Gene — my heart's in my fucking teeth — and I can hear the sea blood within me!"

My own heart thumping, thighs swollen tight — as I lie sprawled, exhausted in my shirt and pants and the sweat keeps pouring off me —

"A Guinness, Gene?"

" — No, no — let me just rest."

"You sure you're all right?"

Nodding, " — You?"

"Fine, fine, just letting the organs find their proper place — a little coronary trip — Good *God*, but that was it! Bloody marvelous, Hagar! Gardens of Kew're probably *still* dancing! O *they* know who it is, all right — bringing back the dance, the old romance — and now the two of us *together* again! *Two* of us, Gene, to contend with! But you're really *sweating*, aren't you?"

"Yeah, I think I could use a bath pretty soon."

"You want to take it now or later?"

"No, now," standing and swaying, "better take it now."

Boyne getting up too, "Right, and I'll help you carry the water."

"Carry the *water?* You mean there's no hot water in the tub?"

"Never was, you get it from the tank downstairs, then carry it up."

"In what?"

"O anything that's handy, pots, pans, sometimes we've even used hot water bottles!" down the long front hall lined with his old erotic paintings, none of Ciara.

"And how many trips does this usually take?"

"To fill the tub? O no more than nine, maybe ten — twenty-five gallons I guess they hold."

"And the water isn't cold by the time you've brought up the tenth pan?"

"No, not really, you only use steaming water. It makes for a nice blend, piping hot on top and lukewarm down below."

"When's the last time you used the tub?"

"O well as you know I don't usually bathe very often, but it's perfectly reliable — an Irish tub. Here, let's find the proper pans," into the kitchen, across a blue tile floor littered with more Guinness bottles, a china cabinet and a red-checkered tablecloth as Boyne eels round the corner into a scullery, "Ah Christ, what a bloody mess this place is and I just swept it out this morning! Let's see: copper pots, pewter pots, tin pots, cups, saucers — Ah, *here* we are!" as he hauls out a couple of large and dented dishpans, "Still seem in fairly good shape."

"And ten trips should do it?"

"O absolutely, of course! These things hold a hell of a lot of water, just don't tip 'em over on the way up, burn those sneakers right *off*, ha-ha!"

"All right, then you go first."

"A little case of the jitters, eh, boy? Well it's you that wanted the bath. See, fill it just to here, not quite to the brim — that's enough, get a good grip — now up we go." Both my hands holding this pan of scalding water with the steam rising. "Easy does it, watch you don't slip on the floorboards." And carefully up the dark narrow stairs. "Should've turned the lights on first, I guess — steady now, one last step — then on round this corner. Still there, Hagar?"

"Yeah, don't stop!" edging precariously into the bathroom toward that wide green tub on lion's paws.

"Right, dump it — and off we go again! Have to keep up a constant rate of speed if you don't want the heat to fade."

Quickly down the stairs and back to the scullery — he's filled his pan and is out of the room before mine is halfway to the brim — passing each other on the stairs, I'm going up, he's coming down, leaning sideways to let me by — as I start down, he's on his way up again.

"Jesus, you'd think we were building the Great Wall of China!"

"Coolie labor, ha-ha!"

The water slowly rising, steam clouding the air.

"You better get in soon, Gene."

"But we've only brought up seven pans!"

"Better get in now!"

"What about the blend?"

"*Hell* with the bloody blend, I'll bring the rest up myself!"

Unlacing these sneakers and shrugging out of my clothes, a soft pile on the cold floor, this bar of Lifebuoy cupped in my hand as I slip a bare toe over the—YOW!! *Jesus*, is that hot! Scalding the skin, singeing the foot. Gotta do it, though. Must. Letting it soak for a while, you masochist, biting my lip—*Ooo! Aahh! Eeee!!* And slowly lowering into it—Christ Almighty, I'm being *boiled* in an Irish tub! My exposed chest shivering and the gooseflesh running up my chin as Boyne comes teetering back through the door.

"Watch your feet, lift your feet—and I'll ease it in down here!—is it hot enough?"

"You *kidding?* I feel like a fucking lobster!"

"Right, well stir it around a bit. The problem, you see, is the tank's too small and may give out at any moment."

"Seamus, will you please tell me what I'm *doing* here?"

"Having a bath in Kew!"

Out and down again he goes.

And back in a few minutes, "This one's cooler, tank's starting to fade—watch it, lift your feet again!" the water splashing in, "Still hot enough for you?"

"Hell yes, it'll be this way for hours!"

"Well let me just close this window or you'll catch your death of cold. Anything else you need, m'lord?"

"No, I'm fine," settling low in the bath.

"Something to drink, squire, while you're floating?"

"No, just a towel."

"A towel? Right y'are, bring you one of mine, sir, me own floral pattern, I'll drape it over the knob," and he closes the door behind him.

Smiling and soaking in this hot, steaming tub with my knees bent as I lather up with the Lifebuoy rub-a-dub-dub—and now back to Carnaween with all I'd ever wanted, all I'd ever dreamed, Boyne's energy, creative support—and this second chance to recapture the past! "Biggest mistake of your *life* leaving here!" as he wheezes out another lively reel on the organ down there. "Never let you down before and have no intention of doing so now!" Limp, redtipped phallus coming up for occasional nosings of air, water over the ears, echoes from the sea. And Ciara — Christ! Still can't believe — He in love with her too? Erotic paintings of my dazzling Dutch colleen — Teri screaming she's a fantasy. So little sex during the last few months, ever since my father died. Gone, those early fun-filled days when we recreated Paris to some degree, the fun wearing off as I kept working in the business and Teri became more demanding, wanting me to break from my parents, and finally couldn't live with me — But could *anyone* live with me? Primed now for flight — wanting commitment, but freedom too — and the fear always returning, my dreams of escape — "Thank God we didn't have kids!" — She wanting two before she's thirty, now twenty-six, but still looking nineteen as on the day I met her: jogging one morning through Central Park not long after returning from Ireland, I was gazing up past Fifth Avenue's tall wall of buildings at a drab, blank sky, dreaming again of rain and grass, trees and paths, when crashing into me around a leafy curve came a green-eyed girl on a gray Arab mare — off she fell and down I went — and as she rose smiling like Sabrina Fair and I helped her to her feet, there was this whinnying collision behind us of horses and saddles, riders and bridles, and squealing fifth-grade girls — "Gene, the point is the marriage has been over for some time now!" — And the next night meeting down in the Village at the White Horse Tavern for cheeseburgers and porter as we huddled together in a backroom booth and Teri, slender blend of lash, gleemouth and glow, told me all about her nineteen-year-old life: growing up in Fargo, North Dakota, dirt poor with a drunken father and a brother who really raised her, three semesters at nearby Moorhead State before running off and getting married to the first boy who asked her — "Just to get to Minneapolis, and that lasted a year (he turned out to be a Peeping Tom), and when I eventually got over that, I packed up my one suitcase and nine pairs of jeans and took a Greyhound bus to New York to study art or really, as I said to myself at the time,

find fame and fortune as a model, but you had to be five-eight
and skinny as a rail, so I wound up teaching riding in Central
Park and then ran into you, the first writer I've ever met, who it
turns out lives just around the corner from the Parke-Bernet!"
And a few weeks later driving up to the University of Mas-
sachusetts for a Pest Control Conference as my father's represen-
tative and sneaking Teri along (my mother already worrying
about my "dating a *shiksa* so much" and Teri increasingly torn
between returning to North Dakota and wanting to stay with
me). In our heated needs and the early days of fall as up the
Merritt Parkway we drove at dusk, our conversation florid and
warm as we sped past leafy Greenwich with its lack of squalor,
snuggles and teasing laughter and, filled with the desire to escape
the car, I went veering off on the embankment, to doff my
sneakers, her loafers, and race hand-in-hand across a dark field of
grass, tumbling and sinking down, kissing and clinging and
fumbling over her breasts and rising thighs, her hips revolving as
she kept sighing and moaning—and her voice suddenly shattering the air: "Gene, let's go back to the car, someone might see
us." And never really accepting her all these years, so wishing she
were another free-spirited Ciara, and now she's filed for
divorce—

BOOM!!!

Jesus, what the hell was *that?*

Boyne lurching headlong through the door, "*Hagar, Hagar*,
let's *go*, we have to get out of here *now!*"

"What *happened?*"

"Water heater blew sky high—bomb was meant for me!"

"What bomb?"

"In the heater, water heater—probably plastic explosive in
the boiler—anyway we'll go to my show by boat!"

"Boat? *What* boat? You have a boat here too?"

"Of course, picked one up in the rushes, be in Chelsea in an
hour, the grand entrance, the two of us together again cruising
down the Thames, singing the whole way in—Ready?"

"Ready, ready!" as I swing dripping out of this bath to towel
off with his floral pattern and, quickly dressing, zipping up my

pants, come bounding down the stairs, the smell of the explosion filling the air — and Boyne tossing me a matching Irish sweater, "Christ, we're going to look like twins, Seamus!" that I pull blinking over my head.

"Through the bloody looking-glass! — O Good *God*, nearly forgot my paintings!" dashing into his studio and back in a flash with an artist's portfolio under his arm, "We're off!"

Outside the wind still blustery and that gray sky gusting along as we go galloping down the towpath, gulls wheeling and shrieking over the trees, and Boyne knifing through the poplars past this damp sloping shrubbery, "See, there's our Donegal trawler and the pier, wharf, or whatever the hell it's called!" to a small white dock with an old bobbing fishing boat some twenty feet long as we broad jump aboard, the deck loudly creaking — a bewildered-looking dragon with its foot in its mouth painted above the wheel, and the Thames seething and receding.

"That the name of the boat?"

" — What? O right, right," *The Good Ship Wino* stenciled on a life buoy, "and the dragon's my trademark, after the *Book of Kells* — be worth a bloody fortune someday!"

A couple of dinghies gliding by the glowing seaside cottages with Boyne crouching low. "And you can really handle this?"

"Of course, I'm a superb navigator, Gene! Clear seas, stiff breeze, zip all about, another Vasco da Gama — do a good twelve, fifteen knots, perfect for escape!"

"But why're they trying to kill you? Will anyone gain by your death?"

"Nobody, I'm not worth a farthing, a bloody sou!"

"But who?"

"*Who, who?* O Laura, I suppose, get Tory free and clear, creditors, old lovers' husbands, IRA or the Prods — "

"IRA?"

"O I made some statements once to the press, 'A plague on both your houses,' wouldn't contribute to their cause — But I'd better get my garb on here — always pays to have on the proper garb!" Boyne fitting a sou'wester over his beret and slipping into a yellow slicker, his grizzled beard ruffling in the breeze, before giving the engine a swift kick as it shudders into life.

"And you really know what you're doing?"

"O *absolutely*, smoothest ride you'll ever have, I'm most adept at nautical things, boats and the like — Well hell, it's in my blood, God bless — I was *named* for an ancient river!" and slamming the throttle forward, we go speeding away with the *Wino* slapping roughly through the waves, "Now where?"

"'Now *where*'?"

"Ha-ha! just testing you, Gene, see if you're paying attention! That's Strand-on-the-Green 'cross there with her bay-windowed houses — no one behind us. I'll just nip round these barriers, buoys, various flotsam and jetsam — never remember if it's right or left, port or starboard, who the bloody hell knows, probably end up at Wimbledon serving for the match! And time to break out the wine!" Boyne reaching under the wheel and holding up a green slope-shouldered bottle labeled with that bewildered-looking dragon with its foot in its mouth.

"This isn't the same stuff we got drunk on seven years ago?"

"Essentially, yes, Flynn and Dungannon's ancient blend, now revived! Threw in half of my savings or Sligo's quids before mice invaded the chateau, our enterprise went defunct — though they still want to buy out my share!"

"I never knew there were vineyards in Ireland."

"O, of course, Glengariff, my mother's home, down the southern coast where palm trees rub branches with bamboo. But Good God, they were drinking wine when the King of Ireland in the sixth century, Murktagh mac Erca, a relative of mine, had his palace set afire by an avenging woman, dove into a malmsey butt to avoid the blaze, and was drowned to close out a dynasty! But here, Gene, use my opener, my phallic corkscrew — there, right!"

Quick spin, the cork popping free and I fill his glass, then mine, to the brim.

"In other words it's the sort of wine given to you in times of stress or under duress by a bearded Celtic satyr! Ready?"

"Ready."

"First swirl it round to bring up the bouquet, plunge in your nose to breathe the aroma, then a brief sip before swilling it down."

" . . . *Wow!*"

"Well?"

"*Jesus!*" still smiling and licking my lips, "This stuff is *nectar!*"

"Didn't I tell you, Hagar? Here," Boyne draining his glass in a gulp, "Ah, that's the taste, frisky, coltish—just a hint of nymphomania—O *great* gulping wine!"

"Yeah, and we'll probably be blind by the time we get in."

"Absolutely! the two of us *together* again—but now, Gene, see if you can come up with a weather report on the BBC, radio's in that compartment."

> ". . . *The inshore forecast from Sheerness to Dover, includ-*
> *ing sea area Thames and the outer estuary: Fresh to strong*
> *northwesterly winds, force five to six, good visibility,*
> *becoming moderate to poor in showers. Gale warnings have*
> *been posted—*"

"O Christ, the seas're whitecap and the winds're twenty knots, toss of the roaring main! Though, of course, boy, what it really means is we're probably in for a bloody monsoon! 'Cause you never believe what these people say, they're always off by a couple of days, like Stonehenge, rattling the bones! Here, let's shut this off—you ready for another swirl?"

"Not right now."

"Yea-ah, well nothing like this wine when the game is afoot, adventure brewing—Come on, just a final toast to lubricate the larynx!"

"All right, last one."

And refilling our glasses as we breeze into clear water, cleaving the waves and under this concrete bridge, waves rocking the stern with the river shapely curving now—and Boyne suddenly singing, "*Gentlemen songsters off on a spree, doomed from hea-ah to eternity!*" the trawler tossing, riding the fierce, churning tide with me bracing one hand against the side—

"*SEAMUS, LOOK OUT!!!*" A giant prow heading straight for us.

"—What? O Good *GOD!!*" and he swerves furiously out of the way, narrowly missing a rusty unmarked tanker, "—*Sons of bitches*, they nearly ran us *down!*" the towering black stern sliding past, spreading a foamy fan in its wake, "—You all right, boy?"

Mutely nodding with gulls shrieking low through the blustery air and my heart still hammering away.

"Ah, but no need to fear, Hagar, with me at the helm—hell, even da Gama ran aground off the coast of Mombasa!" by warehouse walls and power station chimneys, Boyne taking another long belt of his wine under the shadow of Battersea Bridge—"And that's Cheyne Walk up there where Turner climbed upon his roof posing as 'Admiral Booth' and sketched the dawn from his railing! Had himself lashed to a bloody spar—but of course you know that story: four hours in the teeth of a gale on the deck of the steamboat *Ariel* so he could get the desired effect? Even tried it myself once during a thunderstorm, tied myself to the greenhouse, got waterlogged and nearly drowned! But *now*, Hagar! *Now's* the time to do it! Here, boy, take the wheel—" The boat careening left.

"What the hell are you *doing?* We've got to get to your show!"

"Kick danger right in the arse, only way to respond, never give 'em the satisfaction of showing fear, stiff upper lip and splendid erections!" and Boyne goes climbing, clambering atop the cabin in his sou'wester and yellow slicker, "Make the grand entrance and we'll *really* give 'em a show!" with the boat wildly pitching to and fro.

"Seamus, will you get *down!*" as he staggers and hangs onto the flagpole, "You're going to *fall off!*" trying to slow the motors, steady the wheel, and not jar him loose!

"*Nonsense*, boy!!" his chin high, beard rustling, and the whites of his eyes gleaming with that fiery myopic glare, "—Here, you *bastards*, take your best bloody shot—with Runty Billy up there, *Hannibal Crossing the Alps, Burning of Parliament*—and now *The RETURN of Seamus Boyne!!!*"

His chin still high under the billowing sou'wester, gripping the slender pole behind him as I keep struggling with this wheel against the buffeting slap of the waves, spray slicing across my face, "Seamus, get down, will you, before you *kill* yourself, we've gotta get going!"

"—*Going?* Going *where?*"

"To your *show*, goddamn it!" desperately trying to steer her straight rather than go listing crazily about like a toy boat in a bathtub!

"O Jesus, Gene—*absurd, absolutely* absurd my going! We're staying hea-ah, right hea-ah for the evening—take the *Wino* down the Thames past Greenwich and Gravesend and round to Carnaween—Erin's green and fragrant shore!"

"Yeah, OK, OK, but first just get the hell *down!*" The *Wino* angling in toward those houseboats—then back out into the rapidly shifting current, cruisers veering widely out of our way.

"—Who *cares* what those whorish critics say? Never giving us our due, nor appreciating Turner in his lifetime 'n' killing off Van Gogh, Cézanne, Gauguin, and Amedeo Modigliani—"

"Christ, we're really going to *crash* this time!! I don't know how to steer this fucking boat!" easing the throttle back with one hand and still fighting the wheel with the other.

"Such bloodsucking queers they are! Who in the hell *needs* 'em?"

"—But everybody's *waiting* for you!"

"Yea-ah, all my fans and hangers-on, Hagar!" Boyne reaching up now with both hands to adjust his sou'wester—and nearly falling off—blindly clutching the flagpole behind him as the boat keeps thrashing vainly about, "—Ah, the high-wire balance's still thea-ah, boy, like one of those Flying *Wallendas!*" his beard gray-flecked like foam in the dark river light, that manic, ear-to-ear grin, his chin raised high again, and the current sweeping us back toward those jutting rocks and sheer stone wall looming far above—as a helicopter suddenly appears out of the blue with its deafening rotors rattling, "*Down*, Hagar, duck *down!* pretend we've never noticed, are fisherfolk trawling for *cod!*"

"In the *Thames?*"

"Of course — *Irish*, have no idea of direction!" The helicopter hovering low like a bright-eyed dragonfly, then abruptly whirling away. "See, see! Just 'cause I'm paranoid doesn't mean the whole world's not trying to *kill* me!" and dropping to his knees, Boyne quickly clambers down, holding onto his sou'wester, "Treacherous goddamn *voyage*, ha-ha! Surveillance from the skies, MI5 — probably *knew* I was coming by — Right, and I'll take over the wheel now, boy," toward this weird-looking bridge, "Ah, Albert's blazing Tinkertoy!" under we go, "and guide her *myself* to Ireland —"

"Like *hell* you will!"

" — Gene, get your bloody hands *off!*"

Wrestling with him for the wheel as I force it to the left — "No, we're going to your *show!*" — then lurching round to the right, "Seamus, your *Comeback* Show, greatest show of your *career!*"

"*No*, no need to *go!* Surrounded by that world of hyenas all scavenging and waiting to pounce — feeding off people like us, feeding off gossip, off fear and the bad news to salve their own *souls —*"

"But everybody'll be there —"

"*Precisely*, and that's just why going means pinning me *down* and the point, whole point, of my life has always been *not* to be defined just by one's art — this's the *American* way, this's what happens to an artist, what's been happening to *me*, no other reality exists —" The *Wino* now floundering waywardly about. " — But Good *God*, there are far more aspects of a person that — as Courbet said, 'To be not only a painter but a man' —"

"Seamus, *goddamn* it, will you let *go!*" both of us still battling with the wheel through this fiercely surging current, heading once more toward those rocks.

" — And that's why you're coming with me — 'cause in Ireland you can exist in *spite* of your art! You're a man *first* — the artist *always* more important than his work!"

"But you *are* more important, Christ, you've *always* been more important!"

"—Yea-ah, but if I fail now," his eyes shining with tears, "lose my daughter, that's it, nothing more for me to do but join *Turner* up there! Narrowed it all down to this—pinning my life on one bloody *vision*, one bloody *show!*"

"But there'll be *other* shows, other—"

"No, no, not if this fails, lose my girl—no *more!* And I can't go back to that house, to Ireland again without her, without success—I couldn't *face* it again, never paint again, can't take the solitude anymore, being alone—Gene, I *can't* go, I-I don't *want* to go! I don't want to *face* it!!"

"But what'll it matter if you face it or *not?* It doesn't matter to the reviewers, so you might as well go and *forget* about tomorrow, hell with it, and what happens, *happens!* Your appearance's not gonna influence the reviews one way or the other, it's your *work* that counts—and of course you'll paint again, you've been doing it all these years while I let the years drift *by*—"

WHOMP!! The sound of splintering wood!

"*Jesus*, what the hell'd we *hit?*" looking up at the long concrete pier, an oily zigzag of colors coating the lapping waves, "Seamus, you OK?"

"—My whole life wasted, gone astray—O *God*, Hagar, you just don't *know!*"

"Where the hell are we? What, what don't I know?"

"—and now they're taking my *girl* away, my *only* child!" tears glistening down his cheeks, "stealing her from me, I should say!"

"Though we seem to be staying afloat—Seamus, hey easy, take it easy—"

"And I can't do a thing *about* it—*nothing*, not a bloody thing!"

"That's not true, going back next week—But how're we gonna get *up* there?"

"O Mother of Christ, Gene, had all these dreams and marvelous plans for her—"

"—nothing to tie onto—"

"—my wife leaving me when I needed her the most—"

"Maybe those ladders, all rotted away—Well so has mine—"

Boyne still crying and shaking his head, "—And the judge won't care—what the hell's a judge care for shows or lasting fame? Just a façade—thought I could evade it, not have to face it, always figured I had time, more time—O God, I *tried*, Gene, I did, I really did—"

"Seamus, will you *listen* to me!" The sky growing darker.

"—and now I've lost my daughter, lost her *forever!* You have any idea, Hagar, what it's like to lose a *daughter?*"

"Seamus—" easing the throttle forward and gliding on through the choppy water.

"And they give her everything, every bloody thing she wants back there, back where they cut your balls off with a smile! Gene, they're *killing* me! Those bastards back there are *killing* me—but she's *still* my girl and she'll come back—you wait, just wait, one day she'll come looking for me, come seek me out, that burnished little girl—'cause there's a card, have a postcard from her at my house, 'I'll never forget the Museum'—" Bumping hard against a piling, Boyne rapidly blinking and glancing up, "Jesus, where the hell are we? Ah, Chelsea Embankment's up there—then this *has* to be Cadogan Pier—nobody ever find us here!"

"Right, and your show's in Cadogan Square, so let's get going! Though how the hell're we gonna get *up* there, use a pole vault?"

"No, there're ladders, Hagar, *always* ladders!"

"Yeah, all rotted away, pier's probably been condemned," rounding the far end, debris in the water and bollards above.

"So? So much the better—but you worry too much, always worried too much!"

"I'm worried about your boat."

"No fear, just back her in—Here, I'll tell you when to cut it—*Now!* There you go, right, perfect!" and he loops a bicycle chain round a piling, "Knew you were a born sailor all the time!" the boat knocking against these rotting timbers.

"Yeah, but how're we supposed to get *up?* We're still two feet below this ladder, which only has three rungs."

"Well then, I'd best scramble up and tie her down—"

"Scramble up *how?* It's way the hell above us! Listen, there's another ladder down there—"

Removing his slicker and sou'wester, "And I'd better not fall in—'cause you fall in that, Gene, you decompose—nothing lives in there except Godzilla or the Beast from Forty Fathoms, ha-ha!"

"Just be careful!"

The boat riding the choppy swells as Boyne in his tilted beret, Irish sweater, and gray seersucker shorts goes scrabbling up past the missing rungs—and onto that dark, deserted pier with Chelsea Embankment high above, cars zooming by—and not a sound.

"*Seamus?*" as I glance all around.

"—Right *he-ah*, Hagar! And gather up my paintings, would you please, 'cause it's going to pour, really rain—Christ, any minute now!"

"Yeah, well you sure you want to leave the boat here, not worried about thieves, the harbor patrol?"

"Good *God* no, let 'em drink my wine, boy, good business there! Anyway, let me give you a hand, Gene, just lock the galley, douse the hurricane lamps—"

And with my blue raincoat slapping and flapping all about, he lifts me clear, "—So where the hell are we now, Chelsea?"

"Chelsea? Impossible, I wouldn't be caught *dead* in Chelsea, ha-ha!" moving quickly along the pier toward that corrugated tin fence, "Absolutely marvelous entrance, Hagar, sly, secretive, catch them unawares!"

"Yeah, 'bout the only ones who know we've arrived are the gulls and a few water rats!"

"Ah, there!" Boyne opening a narrow flap in the fence, "See, *always* a way out!" and up this covered gangway to the abrasive whoosh of cars and buses rumbling down the Embankment as we go trotting across the road and through these flower gardens, "Good *God*, we're on Cheyne Walk with Turner's pub, The Ship and Bladebone, less than an ass's roar from here—you feel like a drink now, Gene?"

"No, let's just get to your show!"

Flagging a cab to 62 Cadogan Square and round the corner
into the Kings Road with Chelsea flying by outside.

"Isn't that Sloane Square up ahead?"

"Right, right, and I'm in and out: ''Lo, bye.' Whip in, wipe
out—and just look at all those bloody *cars!*"

"Relax, that's only a taxi stand," streaking past Cadogan
Gardens toward a high-windowed Georgian house with
wrought-iron fences and a stucco and latticed façade, "That
looks like it, people going in."

"All of 'em going *in*, ha-ha, then I'm going *out!* See you!"
pushing open his door to hop outside—as I haul him back inside
and slam it shut.

"—Seamus, *Christ*, I'm telling you it'll be over in a flash,
give them the grand entrance!" and we pull up in front with a
screeching splash.

"Grand, ha-ha, yea-ah!" adjusting his beret, "Well hell,
Gene, bugger *all!*" and leaping to the curb, he swaggers flam-
boyantly in.

Lights glowing, faces gleaming, his paintings lining the
walls—

"O he's *HERE*, he's *HERE!!*" "Mr. Boyne is finally here!!"
"We wondered where you *were!*" "Please, *everybody*—Ladies and
gentlemen—excuse me, please, but this is Seamus *BOYNE!!*"

His manic grin, a wave of his hand, Irish music filling the
air—

Jesus, what an entrance!

"Uncle *Seamus!*" a pretty girl kissing his cheek and taking
the portfolio, "We've been waiting so long for these!" then
introducing him to a host of admirers as I keep anxiously
glancing around, feeling the excitement and glow, as though his
show is actually mine—

"Ah, *Hagar*, m'boy, come here 'n' meet all .these aesthetic
people! Gene himself is a poet, a true poet—and my *friend*,
which is *far* more important! God bless us, this is true! But
you've already met Flynn's niece of nineteen, Jennifer Breen,
who's off to Ireland on the champagne flight!"

"Seamus has told us so much about you—"

"And this is Herr Mumble and Dr. Jumble, and they've both come to *buy*, ha-ha! And that's the sensual bride of Dr. J from Roslyn, L.I.—Gloria, yes. Well Gene hea-ah is from Great Neck where the rich people live, came all this way to *guide* me!"

Jennifer's wide eyes staring at me, "Are you Irish also?"

"*Hagar?* Good *God* no, he's an Ivy League *Jew!*"

"O don't tell me you're *Jewish?*"

"All right, I won't tell you."

"No, seriously, I didn't mean it that way, it's just you don't look it at all, resemble the common stereotype, you know?"

"*Ah*, and here're my elegant patrons, Vi and Brenda—Gene, I'd like you to meet the sisters Sligo-Moeran, descendants of Normans, Elizabethans, and Cromwell's conquering army—and the owners of all you survey!"

These two sharply contrasting biddies: one wrinkled and matronly, in a gray tweed suit, with a flat, unblinking stare, tapping a riding crop in her hand, and the other clinging to her flaming youth, wearing a pinkish pastel print and trailing a wispy feather boa, exclaiming, "O Mr. Boyne, we're so terribly, *terribly* excited that you came!"

"Brenda, please!"

Lightly pianoing her fingertips across his cheek, "All this is so stimulating—"

"Brenda!"

"—for I simply *adore* your work," then frolicking merrily around him, "it just opens me up completely—"

Thwack! Vi's riding crop striking her thigh.

"And you still *look* so wonderful!"

Thwack!

"*Smell* so wonderful!"

Thwack, thwack!

"Easy, my dears, easy—But tell me, Jennifer, has the reviewer been here yet?"

"Well John Russell and Terence Mullaly are due any moment, along with Brian Fallon from the *Irish Times*, Guy Brett and Nigel—"

"No, no, I mean the *LONDON* *Times*, Kenneth Clark, only one that *counts!*"

"O yes, well, he's on his way, taking William Gaunt's place, who's on holiday, and he said he would ring up later with his review—"

"*His* review, Christ!" and tossing back a drink from a passing tray, "The critics called Turner's *Snow Storm* a mass of 'soapsuds and whitewash'!" Boyne leads all of them away through the appreciative crowd with Brenda linking herself to his right arm and the busty Mrs. Jumble to his left—

"Gloria, please."

"Gloria, of course! 'For there once was a *girl* name of Gloria who was had by Sir Gerald DuMaurier, and then by six men, Sir Gerald again, and the band at the Waldorf Astoria'—"

"Pardon, but I am Laetitia Marengue," an aging Zsa Zsa Gabor shaking my hand with her slim beringed fingers, European accent, plucked eyebrows, and blue dirndl skirt, "And you are Mr.—?"

"Hagar."

"Yes, well we wondered, Mr. Jagar—"

"*Ha*gar."

"*Ha*gar. Terribly sorry. We wondered where you *were*."

Draping my raincoat over my sleeve, "Well we came by boat, Donegal trawl—"

"By boat? O how charming, by boat. And here—Ordway? *Ordway?* (He is a little deaf, you see.) For Mr. *Ha*gar, a drink, please? There you are."

My hand now holding—what, Ordway? Irish Mist—and down it goes with a smoldering hum as I roam milling round this room filled with gawky, pallid-faced girls, the blood rushing up to apple their cheeks with a soft pink stain—and where the hell is Boyne? Where'd he *go*? Suddenly all alone as I glance about—and what am I doing here, back to my wild salad days, wayfaring Hagar aloft on the wind? Nostrils flaring at the heady gust of stud in the air, "There he goes, girls, get him!" Confidence waning, feeling so uneasy again, a shadow of my former self—No, younger girls love older guys, married guys, guys over thirty. So says Teri—and she ought to know—now faraway in Fargo! Once telling me of calling an old beau, unseen since college, just to hear his voice, and hanging up when he answered. And a whole *world* of girls out there, new generation hopping from bed to bed while I nuzzled, nestled into my wife's warm womb—these chance girls of Chelsea now smiling at me. But what do I say? Offering lines of the fifties? Have no idea how to talk to girls anymore, just grunt and Teri understands. Now back to small talk, the old savoir faire? Hagar, the fairhaired—Still, *whatever* I say and *however* I look, worn and musty in my carefree style, it sure beats the hell out of killing roaches!

And *there's* Boyne, moving upstairs beside Vi and Brenda— and Flynn's "niece," lithe Jennifer Breen, a slim colleen—Come live and dance in Carnaween! Christ, she probably would too!— heading toward that office door. These slender, graceful girls in orange slacks and sandals, fine dark hair chopped at the collar, the gloss of natural make-up—and this passing conversation: "Hi, I'm Mary Rabbit." "What kind of name is that?" "It's Irish, actually, it used to be O'Hare"—as I brush by hopsack, tweed, and summer plaid—a turn of their gaze to suffer my Irish sweater, slacks, and these Adidas sneakers still somewhat damp— and if you've guessed Joyce, James Augustine, madame—no, merely a mask!

A bagpipe's distant skirling up there and Boyne's brilliant paintings here of lovers embracing in a shimmering swirl of sea greens and aquamarines—Jennifer and the stately Laetitia now placing all of Ciara's unframed lusty poses atop wooden runners on those bare alcove walls—And, Jesus, will you *look* at those poses! which no one has ever seen: spread like a centerfold upon a bed, amid a flaming sky of gold and magenta, stroking the insides of her thighs; another holding her girlish breasts, those firm, glistening globes; or playing with herself, eyes closed in orgasm, pubic hair and nipples erect—I'm growing erect! And these BBC accents gasping in awe: "I say, frightfully blonde, isn't she?" "Indeed! Frightfully blonde." And all I did was *describe* her! as I turn away, raincoat cloaking my pants, and go brushing by these swishy men, light laughter, their high-heeled boots, buff-colored crushed velvet suits, dark glasses, and ascots of foulard, hands on hips, limp wrists dangling—can't get through. "Well first of all she was raped when she was thirteen." "By who?" "Freddie." "Then who'd she marry?" "Freddie." "And what does Freddie do?" "Just mooches around the Nag's Head with a boxer and doesn't say boo to a goose—O hi!" his liquid eyes drinking me in, "I'm Henri," offering his fishy hand, "*Enchanté*." All their snickering smiles eager to play—but I'm off the other way—

Ordway tottering past with another Mist—and Boyne upstairs or already fled to the *Wino*, set sail for Erin? No, hearing that thunderous chortle and Dungannon's bagpipes bleating as I wedge on by these candlestands, people stepping aside with a polite shift of their feet—and I'd better go find him *now*! Someone trying to kill him? The crowd oohing and aahing before Ciara's carnal poses, recreated from my words.

Past the whitewashed walls and two-at-a-time up these carpeted stairs, knees thick with wine and Irish Mist, through a small, latticed-windowed room, and down this long passageway leading into a large organ loft and a sprawl of worn and uphol-stered chairs, floor-to-ceiling windows—and a rousing Irish jig gleefully pealing out over a circling crowd with Boyne and Brenda, Herr Mumble, Dr. and Gloria Jumble all in the center dancing away, bagpipes bleating, a *bodhran* beating, and someone with a brogue shouting my name:

"O Jaysus, Mary and José, *Gene*, how the hell've ya *been*?" Flynn's freckled hands slapping me on the back over and over, orange curls and moustache reeling, "It's *grand* seein' ya again!" his chunky little body crammed into brown twill slacks and a tan turtleneck sweater (hasn't changed a bit with that same puggish face!) and holding me at arm's length, "Hell, yer lookin more like a Paddy every day and we're only just arrivin' ourselves!" The crowd still carrying on, vigorously stamping their feet and clapping their hands as Flynn keeps thrusting people into the dance, "—And Gene, haven't seen ya since, where was it now, Dublin or Delgany years ago?" and glancing around, "And here, Lord love him's Dungannon again, the Iceman Coombeth with

his bloody bags soundin' like the parrot house at the zoo!"
Towering Dungannon glowering down, piping a two-note greet-
ing à la Harpo Marx, then letting shrill note sail, wheezing wail,
and squeezing my hand with a strong meaty grip before getting
back to his spirited reel—his bald dome shining, gray eyes
smiling from the face of Eugene O'Neill, paisley shirt open at
the collar, green kilt and sporran, and his left cheek ballooning as
he inflates the bags, festooned with ribbons and a scarlet
plume—"But listen, Gene," Flynn leaning close, "we'll have us a
natter later, since this riotous throng's been clamorin' to hear me
song!" and turning back to cheers and applause, he belts out *"I'll
tell me ma when I go home, The boys won't leave the girls alone—"* as
Boyne, jigging by with his tilted beret, Irish sweater, and those
gray seersucker shorts—"Ah, Hagar, *there* you are! Come join the
Irish frakaa!"—yanks me into this high-spirited dance and
around we go, rapidly blinking, heel and toe, "—*They pulled me
hair, they stole me comb, but that's all right till I get home—*" "Caught
in this sensual music, Gene, like that marvelous sea-rider
Oisín!" feet flicking, kicking out as we keep whirling and jigging
about, "—*She is handsome, she is pretty, she is the belle of Dublin
City—*" and somebody shouting from the wall, "Seamus, which
is your latest work?" "—My 'latest'? Well Good *God*, right *here's*
my latest—old Johnny Thomas, alias Wing Wang Wong, the
father of 'em *all*—" and starting to lower his shorts, "give you a
private showing—" "Seamus, *no!!*" grabbing his hand, "—of the
longest balls in Christendom, a bloody glockenspiel!" "—*Out
she comes white as snow—*" "—Genitalia *glorioso!!*" and guiding
him into a do-si-do, "Ah, but modesty prevents—" as around we
go, "—revealing my Etruscan fig leaf, for I must tap a kidney
now!" the bagpipes bleating, "And Gene," Flynn grinning as I
spin by, "here's a fine girl for you!" flinging someone into my
arms—"Stop!"—Nordic cheekbones, tiptilted nose, straight
blonde shoulder-length hair—*Jesus*, I *must* be dreaming—

   "Ciara?—"
   "My God, Gene—"
   "—what're *you* doing here?"
   "A girl by the name of Ciara Glasheen!"

"—Have you seen those *paintings* downstairs?"

"O that lying son of a bitch!" as we keep on jigging—bearded Celtic satyr, my ass!—staring at her yellow-sweatered nipples, tight blue denim skirt, and that same glorious hair!

"Let the wind and the rain and the hail blow high,
And the snow come travelin' through the sky—"

"—I mean I could not believe what I *saw*—" My dazzling girl before me! still so lovely, hardly changed—someone linking her arm and whirling her left—

"Ciara, just tell me what you're *doing* here!" the jiggling lilt of her breasts, my blonde poetic dream—

"—O I remembered his name from you years ago—" Brenda linking my arm and whirling me right, "—but where is he?"

"She is handsome, she is pretty,
She is the belle of Dublin City—"

"Gone for a sec—You never *knew?*"

"—No, of course not!" sashaying forward and sashaying back, "I have never even *met* him!" the crowd still clapping and stamping their feet, "—And those, those *poses!* Why would anyone *paint* me like that?"

"I don't know," the blonde down shimmering on her arms—Can't tell her, never believe I only described—and the sweat of health glimmering on her brow, what I've missed all these years, her ability to make it all seem possible, be anything I want her to be—and now a second chance to recapture the past? "But what're you doing in London?" as the bagpipes keep on skirling—

"—It is where I live. And what do *you* know about this?"

"Nothing, nothing—You *do?* Milo's here too?" a fast glance over my shoulder—

"No, no—" Herr Mumble guiding her the other way, twirling a pearl-handled cane, "we are divorced. But Gene—"

"You *are?*" Fantastic! "Since *when?*" and linking our arms again—

"O not too long ago—"

Back to Carnaween with all I'd ever wanted, all I'd ever dreamed, writer, wife, "So you've never been to Ireland yet?"

"No," she smiling, "still not yet. Though Milo was once while we were married. But Gene—"

"And would you still like to go?"

"Yes, someday, I suppose—Is that *him*, is that the artist?" as Boyne comes whirling back into the circle, grinning like a horse with his lips curling away from his teeth, and jigging straight up to us.

"Ciara, wait—"

"How dare you—"

"O Suffering *CHRIST*, you must be *her!*"

"—how could you possibly *paint* me like that?"

"You're even lovelier than I'd *ever* imagined! a nymph in the flesh! wondrous and golden like Leda and the Swan, Deirdre of the Sorrows—"

"But I have never even *met* you! Why did you do this, paint me like that?"

"Paint you? *Good GOD*, I'm never going to *stop* painting you—"

"It's so, so—"

"Flattering, I know, captured you completely! 'Cause I'm going to paint you *forever* in the nude with your rosy arse in the air and a host of shamrocks *laced* through your hair—just wait'll you see my sketches!"

"—*What do you think you're doing?*"

And he goes dancing away with her hand in hand, through the crowd and down the stairs!

Boyne

"*She is handsome, she is pretty,*
She is the belle of Dublin City!"
"Will you let me *go!*" — dashing madly along under this showery
drizzle, wet plane trees silverlimned in the lamplight — "Are you
crazy?" — and on into Sloane Square, cars all impatient at the
lights, squealing past over the dark glistening streets — "Where do
you think you're *taking* me?"

"Down to my boat, my Donegal trawler, give you the grand
tour along Old Father Thames by Greenwich and Gravesend
and back to Carnaween!"

"All right, Mr. Boyne, enough is enough now — "

"Seamus, Seamus, the painter Seamus — "

"Yes, all right, Seamus — "

" — who tonight is famous!" as I continue waltzing deftly
along the curb with the Astaire light step and spin, around and
around and pop, pop the cane, the dancer set loose in the streets,
"Bring back the dance, the old romance — Whee, ha-ha!" pir-
ouetting round this zebra post with her in my grasp — and into a
waiting cab, splashing down the Kings Road with this wondrous
girl beside me, "And your hair, like silken sun sifting through my
fingers, so like my daughter's, my lovely Tory — !"

"Your *daughter?*"

"Of course, the same childlike gossamer grain," and I can't keep my hands off her, caressing her taut, Modigliani nape—

"You have painted her also?"

"Absolutely! One of the essential ways we remain close. And your skin is, mmm, like strawberry shortcake, pink and beautifully smooth—"

"Yes, well, I am afraid I am not on the menu tonight."

Letting out a joyful guffaw, "*Marvelous, ha-ha!*"

"You think that is funny, do you? I am not joking."

To Cadogan Pier, down the covered gangway and through this corrugated tin fence, thunder rumbling in the distance— "Ah, the *Wino*'s still here!"

"Look, really now, Mr. Boyne—"

"You can climb on my shoulders or I could use the fireman's carry—"

"—why don't you just post me your sketches?"

"—no, better I take the lead on the ladder and then you follow—as long as you don't run away."

"And why would I ever do that? But really, I think this has gone far—"

As I go stepping gingerly down, the boat bobbing on the stormy swells and moored by that bicycle chain, rungs creaking, breaking—

"Watch out!"

"*O Mother of Christ!*" and plummeting feet first toward the Thames far below, high tide, suspended in time—rapidly falling—and crashing into the water with a cannonball wake! thrashing and heaving wildly upward—I'm still *alive!*—debris all around me, blinking and frantically dog-paddling—awaiting Godzilla or the Beast from Forty Fathoms—"*Help, help, help!!*" raising one hand above the waves.

And Ciara hesitating a moment before plunging in with a perfect swan dive, her blonde hair flaring backwards—a neat nearby splash!—and finally reaching me, her splendid, radiant face growing clear as I let out another bellow of laughter, "*Ha-ha!*"

And she releases her lifeguard's grip, "But you—you *can* swim!"

"Why of course I can! I'm an Olympic freestyler, Junior Red Cross—"

"No, what you really are is a *lunatic*," pushing me under, "out of your mind!"

And grabbing my beret as I surface spouting like Moby Dick, before scrambling swiftly over the gunwale, then hoisting her up—

"You really are insane!" sweeping blonde strands from her eyes with a quick, defiant gesture.

"No, just sensationally sane, dear girl, but come on into the cabin where there's wine and cheese and towels galore, key opens door!"

"Look at me! Look at *you!*" and grinning ironically as I flop the soggy beret atop my scalp, water cascading down, "You don't even have any hair!"

"The surest sign of virility!" and I go ducking low toward the cabin below with boxes, bottles, and paperback books all piled together, "Here, just toss these out of the way, light the hurricane lamp, nice'n cozy, plenty of room," two flat foam rubber cushions on either side against the walls, long, pale blue, to sit on, "And there's even a loo back there, 'cause you'd best get out of your clothes."

"O really? And what do you suggest I wear?"

"Ah, well," gazing all around, "how 'bout my slicker and sou'wester? Love to paint you in those, like Winslow Homer, *Gulf Stream, Kissing the Moon*, or a Degas nude brushing out her hair—and meanwhile, I'll break open a case of wine!"

She shutting the door behind her with a huff as I strip briskly down to the buff and wrap myself in this soft quilted comforter, then shortly thereafter the loo door creaking open and—"*SWEET JESUS!*"—Ciara shaking out her tawny tangles, "What a *vision* you are, like Venus on the half shell, sheer ripeness and bloom—you're all the inspiration I need!"

"*Inspiration?* And what was your inspiration to put me in all those *poses*, drag me away with you here?"

"Feel like Pygmalion with Galatea, Higgins with Eliza Doolittle or Renoir with Gabrielle Renard —"

"But I have never *seen* you before tonight!"

"— which surely calls for, here, a toast of Irish wine!"

"No, I had too much at your show already."

"Nonsense, my dear! And anyway, it's what I put of myself in the painting that counts."

"Then you should have painted yourself, not me! Why didn't you use Irish models?"

"Irish models, Christ! Irish girls won't even take their panties off! For as long as they remain on, they don't consider themselves nude — and therefore, as an artist, I have to imagine, if you will, their furry pubis, mons veneris, soft floral labia —"

"Good, well you go right on imagining because —"

"— and like Turner with Mrs. Booth, Picasso with Dora Maar, or Rembrandt with his beloved Saskia, I'm obsessed with the memories of sexual pleasure, a celebrator not a denyer! But Jesus, you look so cold just standing there, come sit here beside me, all nice'n cozy, Ciara, or nice'n Ciara, cozy."

"No, I'm fine," now sipping her wine, "But you are Irish, yes?"

"No one is more Irish than a Boyne from Valhalla, New York!" as I take a nervous breath, "Do you like the wine?" and she sits across from me, "I once owned the bloody vineyard."

"Yes, it is very good, but you still haven't told me how you could paint me without seeing me."

"I know, great gulping wine, frisky, coltish —"

"And where are these supposed sketches?"

"Would you care to gulp some more, 'cause you seem to be shivering — here, let me give you my comforter," opening it up.

"No, no, that is quite all right."

"O I'm sorry, I'm sorry, I didn't mean it that way — for, really, the fact that you're finally here before me has me feeling so, well, so callow and ungainly, so outlandish and shy, like a, well, like an endangered species, a Block Island meadow vole!"

"A what?" her bewildered, smile, "What is that?"

And hopping down on the floor, holding this comforter around me, "A frightened little mouse who goes whisking and frisking all about, seeking refuge from the world, shelter from the storm—" sniffing through a pyramid of boxes and bottles and paperback books—that come tumbling down on my head, she giggling despite herself, "—and comfort for its paws!"

And resting below her, back against her legs, I take her hands and cradle them around me.

"And can you imagine, once I was so shy, afraid to let a girl touch me—now in this heyday of lust where I play at ram, goatman, anything goes—for I was always a late-developer, physically, athletically, sexually—though not artistically, never artistically—at four I could draw anyone who came into our house, exactly, unerringly so, an extraordinary boy with flamboyant charm, very recherché, as they say, used the same silky roundness to draw my daughter when she was that age, six years ago," sighing and snuggling warm within her arms, "and this feels so like my mother's tender cuddling while crooning Bach's 'Sleepers Awake,' forget my cares, despairs—this is the calmest I've felt in Christ knows when," and turning and staring up into her eyes.

Moored on the lordly Thames, the surging sway and drag of the tide, rainfall, seafare, wind's lash, girl's hair, a tawny shade in this hazy light—as reaching forward, I gently kiss her wine-tasting lips, deliciously overripe—"I wonder how many people you've let see this side of you"—moving onto the cushions and hugging her close in this damp and flickering darkness, my hands fumbling under her chill yellow slicker, my breath in her ear, kissing the lobe, and caressing her hair, warm, intense kisses, roaming over the rise of her breasts, as pink and firm as I'd imagined and the nipple hard as I slowly nuzzle its round persimmon shape, sweet-tasting bud of a nipple, belly button and—*Good God!* after all these years and all those paintings, her warm sleek skin, waiting, working so alone with no escape from that feeling of black despair, and now here before me at last—as I hold her tenderly in my grasp, stroking my hands over her lissome body and kissing her knees, up her thighs, over her furry pubis like wild mountain thyme, mound of Venus, soft floral labia, the mingling aromas of blossom and brine as I keep nosing, cupping her succulent cheeks, and my finger moving inside her, spilling over, widening so, then two, all the while gently licking her clit, stroking her clit, taking it whole and sucking her clit, with her head now thrashing from side to side and she mewing, moaning, her thighs quivering, and she urging, "Come up," as I raise my legs over her mouth, both hands fondling my pulsing organ below, her thighs widening—and my cock now at full mast being softly nibbled under me, feeling her lips up to the hilt, her tongue taunting it, taking me whole in her mouth and sucking up and down and still whining, mewing and feathering my balls, three fingers jammed within her as she starts to come, tensing and arching her spine as I hold on, my tongue probing deeper—and her mouth clenched tight, nip of her teeth, she whining louder and louder, nails digging into my pumping thighs—mind fading and I'm coming too, pouring, flooding out of me, she still sucking, moaning, still coming as I collapse, still humming—and shift to the side under this smooth blue quilt, before cuddling closer in, her fingers caressing across my chest, bald dome—and O Christ, Ciara, you're even better in the flesh! The reality eclipsing the dream!

Turning the hurricane lamp much lower and fondling you within the nook of my shoulder as I cradle you in my arms, "God, you've been an image for so long in my life, and then suddenly here beside me—"

"Yes, and what will I become for you now?"

"—that all I can think of is what St. Augustine said, in that greatest of love lines, 'I just want you to be!'"

She staring with her lustrous eyes, then sighing and blinking, " . . . Curious, no one has ever wanted that from me," as we gently nuzzle and kiss, the rain outside increasing, thunder growing closer, the surging sway and drag of the tide, and I rise slowly to my knees, your thighs wrapping me round, drawing me down—and O Ciara, Ciara, *Christ*, what a wondrous woman you are! as I plunge wetly softly within you, deep within you, your teasing fingers gliding over my hairy chest, down my hips as

I press you close, lacing your hair, silken sifting sun, and on and on—live with you now and paint like I should've every day, Turner and Bach, and the seas at Carnaween—faster and faster, side to side, rainwind silling over the window ledge and the sounds of the river and Chelsea Embankment's road buckle, buses and bicycle bells, a pale light softwashing our soaking clothes, sneakers, and wool socks—O come live and dance with me there! *gallant lovers gaming in a gap of sunshine*, for you're all the inspiration I need, entwined, ensconced, enthralled with all the joy that lies waiting, there in that green, very special corner of the world, high among trees, overlooking the sea!—your cheeks flushed now above the blue eiderdown, wet denim skirt and yellow sweater, panties and halfbra (unneeded to hamper your sensual shape) cast across the wine: soft and gentle under the lily whites with candle lights and lemon tea and morning flesh under the summer me—as our limbs intertwine, suckling your breasts and thrusting away, getting closer, you grimacing, lashes fluttering, to the rhythmic slide and sway of this boat—rain falling all about us, raising you higher, and even faster now, though waiting, holding back with your shrieks and cries—"O Seamus, please, please, I'm so wet! O please, now, now, *now!*"— and come in a long shuddering rush, the sperm spurting from me—your fierce spasms as they recur once, twice, again—and sink headlong together into the muffling silence!

Your warm beating blood beside me, locked in each other's arms . . . To awake soon in Ireland on some rumpled green morning with the seas at Carnaween and paint you in a stunning variety of poses: like Matisse, in transparent Turkish blouses, or in purple like the Queen, rain lashing against the panes, flashes of jagged lightning—

A terrifying crash of thunder, my heart suddenly pounding with panic and fear, all of it returning: trains *roaring* round the bend! shotgun *blasts!*

And abruptly sitting up, "Let's get dressed!"

"Dressed? Why, is something the matter? Where are we going?"

"Well I-I—" sifting through these excess clothes in the corner, "—O back to the party, of course!" tan slacks, stained black sweatshirt—

"You're not tired?"

"Not at all," pulling on a fresh pair of green-striped socks, "You've given me a second breath!" and kissing her tenderly, "a second life! Come, get dressed."

"But what will I wear?" watching her fingerbrush her hair, "I can't go as a vole."

Smiling, "Why of course you can, draped in my yellow slicker!" stuffing the fig leaf and black beret in my pockets, "You'll still look better than anyone there!"

"No, but wait, seriously, why are you in such a hurry now, what *is* the matter?"

And slipping on her damp sneakers as I hold her close, "Ciara, believe me, it has nothing to do with you."

And out to this driving thundershower, following her up another sturdier ladder, and along the covered gangway to Chelsea Embankment.

"Ah, here comes a cab!"

And guiding her swiftly in as he flips down the meter and we go splashing over the Kings Road's glassy sheen to Cadogan Square and this three-story brick townhouse with Dungannon's reedy bagpipes droning out the door, Flynn now singing, "*All you free-born men of the travelling people*," and skipping up these gray-carpeted stairs through the smoke and whiskey-scented air, the room still wreathed with Guinness and Tullamore Dew, and this crowd of well-wishers lustily cheering my return!

Hagar

O Jesus, she trailing behind him, wearing his slicker—and nothing underneath!! That son of a *bitch!* as I go charging across the floor with my gut aching, eyelid really twitching away, and Flynn still singing—

"Ah, Gene—" "*Every tinker, rolling stone and gypsy rover*—" "You fucking *liar!*" shoving him back.

"*Winds of change are blowing*—" "I never lie, you know tha—" "*Old ways are going*—" "Gene, please—" "*Your travelling days will soon be over.*"

"—knowing how much she meant to me!" and hauling off with a roundhouse right, snapping his bald head back—"Will you *stop!*"—my momentum tackling him down, a trickle of blood on his cheek, that manic horsy grin, "—Hagar, what on earth're you *doing?*" rolling over and over, "Phony fucking bastard!" bumping into these upholstered chairs, others shouting—"Mr. *Boyne!*" "Uncle Seamus!" "They're going to *kill* each other!" "Stop them, somebody, *please*—" Dungannon grabbing my arms, "Lemme go!" and people suddenly screaming—

"*FIRE, FIRE!!!* There's a *FIRE* in the *GALLERY!!!*" "The gallery's all *ABLAZE!!*"

"*O Good GOD!!*"

Boyne quickly vaulting to his feet, then racing along the passageway to the bare second floor billowing with smoke and the glare of flames shooting up down there as the rest of us keep crowding anxiously behind, Vi and Laetitia pacing and wringing their hands, "The paintings are *lost*, they're all *lost!*" "Dear Lord!" "*All* of them?" "I-I don't know, we're not sure!" "But they *must* be saved, the new ones haven't even been photographed!!" and Seamus goes galloping down.

"Mr. Boyne, *NO*, you *can't*—" "Somebody *stop* him, *stop* him!" "He'll burn to death!"

O Christ! Nobody moving—*Son of a bitch!* heading after him—waving, coughing, eyes burning, sirens braying, "—I can't see a *thing!* Seamus, get *OUT* of here, damn it!!" and retreating blindly through this thick choking smoke, tears in my squinting eyes, fire engines pulling up outside—

"There he *goes!*"

And banging open this latticed window, rain barreling down, hoses blasting—as he leaps into the fire chief's car, a painting under his arm, swerving onto the curb below, tires spinning, blue lights flashing, then speeding off toward Sloane Street, "Where the hell're you *going*, you madman?" on the wrong side of the road!—and another car behind him? O Jesus!

Sprinting back along the passageway to take these stairs two-three-at-a-time and on out the door—really going to kill himself now or be killed, someone starting that fire!—over this rainslick pavement, a fading screech of tires, and into Sloane Square with no sign of him, traffic wheeling past—and where the hell'd he go? looking left and right, back to the *Wino?* Christ Almighty, my breath heaving so!—chasing my father in the rain, *Boyne wildly jigging by with his beard and beret,* everything falling apart in my hands, losing him again! traffic flying by—*O my father, raccoon eyes squinting in the sun, your double chin, reaching back for you, reaching out for you*—and I'll never catch him now, out on that stormy river—

Boyne

"*CRAZY*, Good *God*, Billy, *I* told you it was *crazy*, absolutely *CRAZY*—" the *Wino* seesawing desperately through these monstrous waves, thunder and lightning, "—nothing to do now but steer for the Tate and hang this last bloody painting *myself!*"

Force six winds and torrential rains—a steadily driving downpour—rising on white crests, cascading into dark troughs, "Never will I see my daughter again—" a stinging spray lashing across my face, "nor *Ciara* again—for as soon as I hang this portrait of her, now charred round the edges and freed from these stretchers (all those people rushing about in the smoke trying to rescue my work), Billy, I'll hang *myself* as well!! Discovering my genius long after my death, but denying my struggles during my lifetime—*O Mary and JOSEPH!*—"

A tidal wave of water knocking me sprawling!! clawing and frantically clinging to the gunwale—

Down, down, we're going *DOWN!! The Drowning of Seamus Boyne*—bells tolling at Lloyds of London—and my helpless little craft hurtling round and round like the *Pequod*, farewell the Ancient Mariner!!

Hagar

Trudging up this gray flight of stairs with the smell of fire still in the air as Flynn, Laetitia, Vi, and the rest all come hurrying toward me:

"Gene, what *news?*" "You *find* him?" "Is he *all right?*"

Shaking off this rainy spray, "No, no sign of him and the boat's gone, God knows where!"

"O dear Lord!"

"And where's Ciara?" looking around.

"Thought I just saw her."

"He's not dead! I'm *sure* he's not dead!"

"How do you know?"

"I just know!"

"Probably only gone back to Kew!"

"We've been calling out there —"

"O those bumblers!"

"The firemen?"

"No — I mean, yes, for nothing's survived, paintings, frames, furniture!"

"But I'm sure he's all right —"

" — has always had nine lives!"

"But he could really kill himself now — or be killed!"

"What?" "Who, Gene?" "What are you saying?"

"Someone's been trying to kill him," and slumping down into this upholstered chair, exhausted now and aching for sleep, legs lumpish, weighted, sleepy-needled feet, like a piece of old luggage flung around London as all of them keep milling about me.

"Gene, listen, why don't ya stay here for the night, 'cause there's a spare bedroom upstairs?"

"And the reviews should be comin' any minute."

"*Times* promised they'd be calling."

"Right, Clark, Kenneth Clark this is—" The phone stridently ringing, "That must be him!" as everybody goes chasing about helter-skelter for a well-positioned seat, Jennifer crashing into Laetitia, Vi colliding with Brenda, Gloria with Dungannon, Herr Mumble with Dr. Jumble, "Mother of God, will someone pick the blasted thing *up*!" and Flynn, bounding quickly over the sofa, plucks the receiver into his hand, "—Ah, Miss Binton, right!" reeling in the looping cord, "From the *Times*, of course! Ready with Lord Clark's review? Ah, that's grand, grand! And would ya be so kind as to hold on a tick?" then furiously signaling to Dungannon ("She's goin' to read it aloud!"), who flicks on a nearby intercom as the rest of them gather around.

"Ready, Mr. Flynn?" her echoing BBC voice.

"Right y'are, darlin'."

"'With a fiery light swirling in a great vortex of color, the paintings of Seamus Boyne's new show at the Sligo-Moeran inevitably call to mind the work of Turner again. Yet his paintings are realized with such an intense degree of feeling and control that their forms, though obviously derivative, acquire a vivid personal dimension and more than survive their influence—most notably the splendidly erotic nudes or the couples in naked embrace. Here there is a similar explosion into color as a field of light and the treatment of paint simply as paint, many of the solid objects consumed in a brilliant, shadowless radiance. Yet the mood remains sensual and warm, shattered and melting and filled with the passionate breath of phantoms, his goals seemingly far more intimate than epic (recalling Turner's Petworth period and those private sketches that Ruskin burned). An altogether astonishing exhibit of a remarkably original genius.'"

"*O Jaysus, Mary and José!!*" Flynn ecstatically beaming — with the rest of them cheering and hugging each other — and his eyes growing glossy, "Well we've *got* to find him now!"

Boyne

Writhing, foamy seas and the *Wino* going down with this gray rain slashing across my bows — toss of the roaring main, run into another tanker bound for Bahrain or the pleasure boat to Kew! — rolling my portrait into a tighter tube and under my Irish sweater — as we keep listing and perilously drifting toward those jutting rocks and seething waves — fall in that I decompose, never paint Ciara or Tory again, my life turning out differently, ravaged by Godzilla and the Forty-Fathomed Beast! — must've sprung a leak — nothing left but to break into the Tate and hang this last bloody painting *myself* — then end it once and for all! Nearing the river wall, that emergency pier — not sure I can reach it, clutching her portrait in my fist and lifting myself onto the gunwale's sloping side — about a two-foot jump or watery grave — NOW!

— and leaping out into space, over the darkling waves like that marvelous sea-rider Oisín —

Skidding, my hand *smacking* the wall, the tide sloshing across my green-striped socks — but still hanging on to my painting!

And looking back as the *Wino* goes sinking and bubbling down like the *Pequod* in a surging wake!

And where the hell can I go? Cold and clammy and wet to the bone, have to find someplace to sleep, need to dry off — no idea where Ciara lives, don't even know her last name! *Damn!* Gloria staying at the Savoy, Jennifer flying out tonight, Vi and Brenda—?

Or Laetitia's Belgravia flat—handed me her address, here, somewhere on this soggy slip—and swiftly up these metal steps to hail that passing cab!

Hagar

—*Boyne wildly jigging by with his beard and beret, nakedly swaying to an Irish reel — a massive wave crashing in, swallowing him up, he dying, my dream dying, can't get to him in time! — as I go racing out of my parents' house — God, don't catch me, old weathered walls, hallowed halls, stumbling down these steps, dark shadows right behind me, all my failures lost in his eyes, the aching weight of this pain and sorrow, so hard to breathe — O my father, images of you appearing, disappearing, reaching back for you, reaching out for you — fading away, flailing like a beached fish on the floor — heart pounding, bursting, running headlong through these dark, scary streets, so wet and cold — Daddy, Daddy! Where are you? working late in the office again, running to find you there, splashing through the puddles toward that blinking neon bug sign — And he's not there! I'm all alone, always alone, never there when I need him! huge black clouds closing in, disappearing — O help please, please, please HELP —*

"No! No! No! No!"

Sitting straight up like a shot, panting with the sweat pouring off me and staring out at this dark, drifting room, grayish light, French windows drizzling — Boyne, Ciara? *Where the hell AM I?* Flynn, Dungannon, London —? Vi and Brenda's townhouse! — and still so scared, my heart hammering, been running away *all* my life! Both of them gone — and my fears of the dark, childhood fears, Teri holding me, hugging me all these

years, but she's sure not holding me now! — and maybe never
again! Ciara gone God knows where! with me fleeing to Ireland
through flung nets, and the dream still back there! — as, leaning
forward, soaked in sweat, I keep staring at my reflection on the
drizzled panes: mop of floppy hair glistening in profusion, nose
with its Roman bump (a wild and rowdy brown bear singed by
the summer), and my father's raccoon eyes — Boyne convincing
me to stay, he painting, me writing, "Christ, life is *leaping*, boy,
never a lying down!" Finding other comforts, other joys — and
not what others wanted me to be. The tyranny of their image,
their fair-haired boy. So self-conscious, eager to be accepted, so
busy, keeping pace. Everyone's favorite, the happy-go-lucky, All-
American, glad-handing Haig. And my father saying, "When I
was your age I had the same thoughts, the same ideas, but you'll
see you'll change, everyone goes through phases like that. You'll
look back later and see how silly your ideas were." My father, a
slope-shouldered Ralph Bellamy with distinguished graying
temples and double chin — could be a banker, a broker, a wealthy
tycoon — with his six-in-the-morning-to-seven-at-night-and-
most-Saturdays' dedication to the business, and golf his only
pastime, mainly for business contacts. At Glen Oaks Sunday
mornings feeling small among the rich Jewish barons: "I played
in a threesome with Dr. Kronefelt of Mount Sinai Hospital and
Lee Greenberg, who's vice-president of Burlington Mills. These
are big men." On his upstairs desk — now mine — three gold
cups, one from Grossingers and two from Glen Oaks, Scotch
Foursome winner, 1948, and Class C Driving Champion, 1949.
His 150-yard-straight-down-the-middle game, thousands of
lessons and just barely breaking 100. "They're having a cookout,
Gene, next Wednesday night, a barbecue at the club. You wanna
go?" Shaking my head no and my mother saying, "If he doesn't
wanna go, don't force him." And rarely going, hating that garish,
all-Jewish club. Like that scene at lunch last time I was there:
gilded-haired mommas in gold sandals and peacock shades
shoving each other aside to get their hamburger: "It's *mine*. It's
mine. I was here *first!*" All those aged women, tanned and
wrinkled and looking like rhesus monkeys, calling each other

"girl," and their husbands, financiers, captains of industry, in pastels and tasseled shoes, out on the links cutting strokes off their scores after another successful season of soaking blood from the dollar! And my father never quitting, coming back Sunday afternoons following a steam and a shower and a glad hand to all with, "They were all there. All the sons were out with their fathers. The only one who wasn't there was you." All those sons and friends of mine moving on from Jewish fraternities to the golf clubs with the same rules, segregated and holding away—and asking him once was he ever ashamed about being an exterminator and he answered, averting his eyes, "O sure. It bothered me, the jokes. But you get over it, you get over it." Really such a shy man, my father, underneath it all, starting Hagar Pest at twenty-six, married at thirty, and avoiding intercourse during the courtship because it wasn't the "right" thing to do, ranting if I came out of the shower without a towel, "Put something on! Cover up your business!" or hastily shutting the bathroom door whenever I found him shaving in just that old-fashioned undershirt, and thinking he would retire at fifty, then at fifty-five—

And *O God!* the tears now flowing out of my eyes and swallowing hard!—and I'm still sweating besides as I keep on crying—everyone crying at his funeral except me!—and all these years, the haunting fact of two lost children, one daughter, older than I, living a day and a half, and a younger son surviving with a frail heart and one hand for less than three months—and overly healthy me with 20/10 vision and never a broken bone, their "Tarzan," lone joy—and the criticism in his eyes when I didn't reach perfection, his list of expected achievements: going to Harvard first instead of Cornell, a four-letter athlete, marrying a beautiful, extremely wealthy Jewish girl, coming into his business, and settling down safe and secure in the suburbs, joining the Shriners, the Masons, the UJA, well-thought-of and religious in the community, and bringing up a brood of well-liked, good-natured children who at birth are enrolled at Harvard and at age three stroll across the ranch house lawn clad in crimson T-shirts—still crying, *Jesus!*—as I moved increasingly away from his dreams: the word "Dad" catching in my throat, always a wince when said, and those last few years in school searching for someone to spur me on, professors, writers, friends, till I finally ran into Boyne, his house of Carnaween, and Ciara coming over, following my dream, my father had his false-alarm stroke, and Ciara married Milo.

Boyne

Warm wet licking tongue, flicking slick pinkish tongue twining over my chest and shoulders, and all but bringing me, who's now sublimely erect in Belgravia, to the maddening, swelling, blissful brink of — *"Who? Where? WHAT is it?"*

"O I am sorry, I did not mean to wake you, Mr. Boyne," Laetitia crawling in beside me on this hide-a-bed, "but you are so beautiful when you sleep."

"— Laetitia, no, please stop!" Those falling gargoyles fading, along with Herr Mumble —

Her face foreshortened by passion: plucked eyebrows, wide mouth lustily grinning, her musky odor filling the air, "You have brought all the warmth and tenderness of your work into my home, Mr. Boyne, or Seamus, if I may call you that?"

"Yes, well, I — "

"And give you a little rub here, and here, and *here*, kootchie koo?"

"— Laetitia, no, please, I'm ticklish — Ha-ha! *stop* it, don't you know — *Wow*, ha-ha! — how many accidents're caused under the lily whites? Come on now, this is getting — "

"O let me just smell you!"

"What're you — Laetitia, what on earth are you *doing?*"

"Smelling you."

"Under the arms?"

"It's clean sweat, a man's sweat, Seamus — I adore the smell of a man, sniff, sniff!" her hands stroking across my stomach and down my thighs to fondle my cock, "And you are so immense now!"

"Yes, well as Flaubert said, 'I always salute the morning with an erection,'" sitting upright, "But listen, Laetitia, I need to ask you, where do I know Herr Mumble from?"

"Mmmm — see how he throbs! Herr Mumble, Mumble? You don't mean Herr Mündel?"

"Yes, yes, that's him! Who is he?"

"My second husband. Why?" still cuddling and fondling me.

"Well he may be trying to kill me."

"Otto? O no, no, no, never — though, yes, maybe that could be. He follows *me* around everywhere, so possibly he —"

"But I've never even *touched* you!"

"No, not until now, mmmm!"

The phone ringing — *Suffering Christ!* "Aren't you going to answer it?"

"Why? Should I?"

"Never know who it might be."

"So? These veins are so blue —"

"Well it might be your second husband or the police."

"O, all right. Yes? Hello, hello?" and she replaces the receiver.

"Who was it?"

"No one. They hung up."

"Good *GOD!*" jumping out of bed, "There's nowhere to hide!"

"Seamus, what is it? You're as white as a sheet."

"*Sheet, sheet!* That's it! Up, Laetitia, up!" and stripping the top one off with a bolero sweep.

"What are you *doing?*"

Then draping it all about me, "I've just had a *marvelous* idea — I must get to Harrods *now!*"

Hagar

The window goes blonde slowly, soft sleeves of sound — *Teri?
Ciara?* looking anxiously around — and no one here beside me! as
I keep on blinking and yawning with little if any sleep — running
through the rain after Boyne, my father, things I can't control,
accept, my fears, failings, own death — for what? from what? what
the hell for? Boyne's art, success, what I've wanted all these years?
To sell the business and write about what I know. But what do I
know? My father, Great Neck, the world I grew up in? Or a
second chance with Ciara? She and Boyne balling their brains
out, she begging for more — but if he's dead, she's mine — no, no,
what am I *saying?* Not even sure anything happened! Everything
so bizarre, she naked under his slicker, like they both fell in the
Thames? Who knows with Boyne! Probably just showed her his
boat, went to a pub — then why'd she leave? Embarrassed at
seeing me? Damn it, I'm not going to *lose* her again! Got to find
her now, *both* of us find Boyne — but where the hell is she? — as I
hop out of bed at 8:45 and go stumbling into the bathroom,
hands on hips, pissing in the bowl — and a cold splash of water
bristling me awake as I stare into the mirrored eyes of my father:
raccoon eyes, which are my own — then quickly shrugging into
yesterday's clothes, Irish sweater still somewhat damp, go hus-
tling down the stairs to where Flynn, sitting at a long glass table

with the morning paper spread out before him, nervously traces his orange moustache.

"Any word?"

"Just had a call, someone saw the *Wino* go down—"

"Christ Almighty!" pounding the wall and pacing around.

"—but there was no sign of a body."

"So where the hell can he *be?*"

"Lord only knows! And to make matters worse, wait'll ya see this lot, all these critics, Russell, Goseling, Melville, Terence Mullaly, fallin' over each other in praise, all of 'em fuckin' sensational! Here, Russell, this is: 'Mr. Boyne's lusty chromatic fantasies yield brilliantly arousing effects,' or Mullaly: 'Nothing more to say except go see one of the wonders of the modern era!'"

"Fantastic, and now he's probably knocked himself off!" still pacing back and forth, "But if he *isn't* dead and wasn't out at Kew, where else could he be?"

"I haven't got a clue."

"You know where Ciara is?"

"Ciara? O I think I heard Laetitia say somethin' about her goin' to the Royal Court in the mornin'."

"Royal Court?"

"Royal Court Theatre in Sloane Square, just down the road—"

"Right," starting down the stairs, "well I'll be back later, so leave word if you've heard anything."

"I shall indeed, Gene!"

Nearly nine already as this taxi goes careering around Sloane Square toward the Royal Court Theatre, and there she is, wearing a tight white sweatsuit—Just be with her, any excuse to be with her now!—coming out the front with her sungleaming hair, and we swerve to a stop before her.

"God, you look incredible!" slamming the cab door behind me.

"—Gene, what are you *doing* here?"

"I didn't know you were acting. Did you get the part?"

"If I did?" Ciara seeming so edgy, embarrassed, "They will let me know. My accent may be too thick."

"Yeah, and where did you go last night?"

"Well, I left when you started fighting, it was so ridiculous!"

"And where's Boyne?"

"How would I know? Why, are you still trying to kill him?"

"Then you didn't see the fire?"

"Fire? What fire?"

"There was a fire in the gallery, Boyne's disappeared, may've drowned, his boat sank—"

"O dear God!"

"—all his paintings were burned, the reviews were sensational—so come on, you have to help me find him!"

"*Me?*"

"Yes!"

Ciara walking on, "Gene, I have not the slightest idea what you are talking about, but I had enough craziness last night and now I am going to jog, I don't want to think about it anymore."

"*Jog?*" hastily chasing after her, "Jog *where?*" and down the Kings Road, "Ciara, will you *listen*—" trying to keep up with her, "Where're you going?"

"Just up here there is a track at the Duke of York's Headquarters."

"But why?"

"To exercise, stay in good shape."

"But you're in great shape!"

"Not 'great' enough, apparently! I have still to lose another half stone."

"Sounds like you live in a quarry."

"Hello," Ciara moving quickly through the military gate, the elderly guard waving her in—with me right behind her.

"Ciara, will you *wait!*"

She breaking into a leisurely trot, "And why is Boyne so *important* to you?"

"'Cause you can't let him die, have somebody kill him! Be like losing Picasso, Van Gogh, Cézanne—for Christ's sake, will you *stop* already!" coming around the far turn of this cinder track with the gulls soaring and the sun pouring down through the fluttering maple leaves, " — And why am I always running *after* you — in the Louvre, here — ?" side by side down the straightaway, " — How many laps do you do?"

"Today I do three."

"Two *more?*"

"Yes, and sprint at the end."

"No way!" by this low brick wall, "OK, Ciara, I'll make you a deal — "

"I am not dealing, I'm running."

" — I'll sprint the end of this one with you if you promise to come with me after — ?"

"You are insane!"

Along the inside lane, legs aching, arms pumping, all this running, playing, chasing — thirty-one now, not twenty-four! — And Christ Almighty, I'm never going to *make* it, coronary assault: *Found dead on Chelsea cinderpath, one Eugene Hagar, late of Great Neck, sprawled flat out, face contorted, in a tortured reach for his dream, beside him sprinting —*

"*Now!*"

Toward the far turn again — and Ciara running so well, so love to see — a girl who runs well — not all awkward, arms and legs flailing — but girlgrace, flowing muscles, bulging calves — she leading by a yard — and I have to beat her, my competitive urge — "I haven't done this in years — " "Well, we are not who we were" — faster now, my heart really pounding with twenty yards to go, she still leading — and turning it on with my last lap kick, Roger Bannister breaking the four-minute mile — here I come on the outside lane, grimacing, gritting my teeth, straining — passing her down the straightaway — leaving her behind and crossing the finish line a yard ahead — as she continues on and —

O JESUS!! gasping — heart pumping so *fast!* bursting through my chest! — and sinking to my knees, fear in my throat, eyes! — *I'm going to DIE!!* — My father's stroke, flailing like a beached fish on the floor — this's how it *feels?* Can't breathe — heart totally haywire, slack mouth hanging open — salt taste, drenched in sweat — can't die now, have her see me like this —

God, *breathe! breathe!! Keep* breathing!!! — and Ciara still running smoothly, her long lean strides, breasts' light bounce, blonde hair flaring in the breeze — and sprinting across —

" — O good, this last lap was — *Gene?*" she hurrying back, "What is the *matter*, you look so white!"

" — First time — " still panting, sweating, and kneeling forward, " — was ever scared — "

"You are not used to it, yes. Here, come sit down here and rest."

"I know — but no sleep last night and — always before — never worried and now — *Jesus!!*"

"Just rest, rest," Ciara gently wiping my sweaty brow, "you can talk later."

"No — I'm all right now," so queasy — and still breathing deeply, "Christ — feel so stupid, like a fish, beached fish — gasping for air!" leaning back on the grass, "Before — just pushed on, never say die, heart attacks, strokes — ridiculous, for old guys, but really, I thought, God — I thought I was going to have — *Wow!* have *something*! First time I ever felt, you know, thirty-one — don't know why."

"Because you *are* thirty-one. And it is very warm today and obviously you are not used to it."

" — No, it's more — " taking another deep breath and staring out at the blurry track — "it's more than that — " coming into focus.

"Are you feeling better now?"

" — Mostly fear, I guess — of death, thoughts about death, nightmares, everything exploding — O *Christ!* — let me just catch my breath!"

"Yes, well wait, Gene, take your time," and Ciara smiling as she brushes the hair from my brow, "Though you should never have run with me."

"Run after you is more like it, The Menopause Mile!"

"No, you did not do so bad, considering."

"Considering what? I almost died or that I'm old and paunchy?"

"O not so old, and maybe just a little — no, I am only teasing you now."

"God, Ciara, here I've been running, dancing, posing, even sucking in my gut — been trying so hard to look young for you, I'm going to *die* in the process!" as I finally stand, regaining my balance, "But now you'll help me find Boyne?" and we cut across the cinder track.

"Yes, yes, now I will help you find Boyne — though I am not sure what I can do."

And on toward the gate with my throat so dry and my blonde glimmering girl beside me again — O Ciara, so needing you now, right now, poetry and song, your life with me: halcyon days, Hagar whirligigged and ran his heedless ways, Aer Lingus lifting us away to — where? "And how long have you been acting?"

Ciara walking briskly along, "Since we were divorced. Remember I had been acting in Holland before I came to Paris?" and we go trotting across the Kings Road.

"Right, right, well we've hardly had a chance to talk, tell me about your life for the past seven years," back into Sloane Square, "So you live by yourself here in London?"

"Yes, though I am staying for the moment with the nuns."

"The *nuns?* You're becoming a — ?"

"No, no!" Ciara giggling and laughing — brightly flashing, her front teeth's slight charming overlap — and going on to explain that her nearby flat in Pimlico is being painted, so temporarily she has moved in with two nuns who live below.

"Below? I see, well what happened with Milo?" turning up Sloane Street, my mind a blur, a swirling daze as I keep staring at her hair of Scandinavian shine —

"Well he is an executive now at ITT, we were divorced in June."

"What happened?"

"O, he wanted me to be his doting little wife and support his career, 'ascend the corporate ladder,' as he would say, while I suffocated in his stuffy world, that Bloomsbury flat. I was like a statue or figurine, something on the shelf to be dusted off during the day and then be all bright and cheery and precisely in place when he came home! Dear God, when I think now, I would sit for days on end on that damask sofa forcing myself to leaf through the *Tatler* or *Elle*, or doing crossword puzzles, clipping different recipes, until one night I said to myself, 'What are you *doing*, doing with your life? I would much rather take care of someone than keep living like this!' I thought I would go out of my mind just sitting there, and finally walked out and left his dinner to defrost by itself, nearly burned down his precious homestead! And now here I am back at acting again, nervously waiting for my first part at the Royal Court, while breaking free from this marriage."

"And all these years, Ciara," approaching Cadogan Gardens.

"Yes, and you are how old now, you said, thirty-one?"

"Not as young as I used to be."

"Well you seem to be in fairly good shape for someone your age."

"Obviously slowing down, can't go to his left anymore, fans—"

"I know, I have seen how very slow you are!"

"—you young kids taking over."

"Shall I give you my arm, old fellow?"

"O get out of here! Anyway, would you really've come to Ireland then?"

"What? O, when I wrote you, you mean? Yes, I would."

"Were you sure I'd marry you?"

"I don't know, I suppose so. But that was before your letter that you had to go home, you didn't know for how long, and then Milo came back—remember he always was going off to Liechtenstein on those Intelligence missions of his?—I didn't hear from you and all of a sudden he asked me to marry him, we went to Holland for the wedding, and then moved here to London. But now you are living in Ireland too? I thought—"

"No, back in the States."

"And you have kept on with your writing?"

"Here and there. I'm in business, took over my father's—"

"But I thought you hated that."

" — I do, *still* do."

"And have you ever married, Gene?"

Nodding as we enter Cadogan Square.

"Do you have any children?"

"No," nearing the red brick townhouse, "Do you?"

"No, Milo never wanted them. And what is your marriage like — Dear God, I can smell the fire from here!"

"It's probably over," knocking on the front door — that opens — no answer, and on up the stairs, "Hello, anybody here? Flynn? Dungannon? Vi, Brenda?" looking all about, "Guess they've all gone out — " The phone ringing. "I'll get it," hurrying across to the alcove, "Yes, hello?"

"Pardon?" a familiar, agitated voice, "Who is this?"

"Gene. And who's this?"

"O Mr. Hagar, please, I am terribly sorry I did not recognize you but this is Laetitia Marengue. Is Mr. Flynn there or the sisters Sligo-Moeran?"

"Nobody's here."

"O *no*, and Mr. Boyne has just left!"

"He's *alive?* Just left for where?"

"Harrods — "

Ciara now whispering beside me, "Who is that?"

"(Laetitia). *Harrods?* But why — ?"

" — dressed as a sheik and I am extremely concerned about him!"

"So am I! Listen, we're leaving for Harrods right now, so I'll speak to you later then."

The two of us cantering back down the stairs — and nearly colliding with Flynn coming in the front door.

"Ah, Jaysus, Gene, Ciara — and will you look at this girl, so pretty she'd make any hour sweeter!"

"Yeah, well listen," spinning him about, "we gotta get going — " and quickly outside again.

"Goin' where?"

Pushing him ahead, "We can take your car — Boyne's still *alive* — "

"Mother of Christ!"

"— and on his way to Harrods!"

"But stop, stop!" Flynn skidding to a halt.

"Why, what's wrong?"

"I just heard over the BBC that the paintings *weren't* destroyed but rather're bein' held for ransom!"

"*Ransom?* What kind of ransom?"

"Didn't say. I know, 'tis all of it exceedingly strange!"

Boyne

Speeding through Saturday morning London traffic in the plush leathery comfort of this Austin cab and I'm unraveled, umbilical anew! with vibrant colors clashing, whirling textures massing across my mind as I apply a final smear of this bronze stain to my glossy cheeks — looking like Auda abu Tayi, sheik of the Howeitat and legendary Bedouin chief! Everyone trying to shed their own skins, cast off this mortal coil: Monet turning into a water lily, Cézanne a rocky landscape, Van Gogh the paint itself (the lead probably causing his madness) — and now me into Lawrence of Arabia, my headdress wound round with a gold sash cord and deftly fashioned by Laetitia, sunglasses, and one of her king-sized sheets — she pleading with me to stay, "O please come back to bed!" — this Aer Lingus bag at my feet filled with a fast change of clothes, cold cream, napkins, her £10 note in my pocket (can't afford to be recognized, the need for disguise with all of London as well as assassins hot on my trail) —

And approaching Harrods now with its brightly flapping flags, huge six-story terra-cotta building crowded with customers as, cruising down the narrow block, we swerve to a sudden stop!

And I come billowing out with my bedsheet-robe flowing in the breeze and under the scalloped awning, by the Harrods guard, a beefy sergeant-major in visored cap — being ogled by children, women in flowered hats — and up these marble stairs to sample some figs and dates, past Wurlitzer organs and Steinway grands, Wedgwood blue and Doulton china, and into this world of hardware for a hammer, nails, and a coil of manila rope, then on through *Kitchenware* and *Garden Care* and a flotilla of *Sporting Goods* —

And Good *God!* that's it: Just look at this one-man *canoe!* Nobody ever suspect — perfect transport to the Tate! My Irish one knocked off by a shotgun's shattering blast — £35 — But hardly any money left, so there's only one bloody thing to do —

"Might I be of service, sir?"

And nearly *leaping* out of my sheet! — as I glance swiftly around at this mousy little man in his gray pinstripe suit — and launch into my Iraqi accent:

"Ah yes, please, begging your forgiveness now, but I am interested, you see, in the purchase of this — how do you British say — canoe, yes? as in gnu, cuckoo, pooh-pooh, ha-ha, touch of Arabian humor there!"

"Quite."

A lithe, well-groomed woman in a bright orange suit passing by, "Any problems, Mr. Mortlake?" and adjusting her horn-rimmed glasses.

"No, no, perfectly all right, Miss Hynde. Proceeding quite nicely, thank you."

"Allah be merciful, such a *lovely* flower!" bowing with a flourishing kiss of her hand — and almost losing my tilting headdress! "Truly a splendid-looking woman. Older, yes, but as it is written, which of us can escape that, you know? As we say in my country, 'To meet a charming woman is even better than to trick the camel trader.'"

"Is that from the Koran?"

"If not, then it should be."

Miss Hynde nervously tapping her glasses into place and, with a lacquered smile, goes strutting away.

"But please excuse my babbling, sir, for I have chosen this six-foot-long, one-man, green fiberglass canoe from Twickenham here." Mortlake nodding and moving behind the counter. "Though there appears to be a slight defect with this particular model. I wonder, might you have another of the same design in stock?"

"Quite. And will this be a charge, sir, or—?"

"O yes, charge, by all means, charge! I delight in the charge, like your Light Brigade, ha-ha!"

"Certainly, Mr.—?"

"Tayi. Auda abu Tayi, of the Howeitat!"

"Very well then, sir, I'll just get a fresh one from the back, shan't be a moment."

"Words alone cannot express my gratitude—"

And he disappears into the stockroom—as I raise the canoe boldly over my head, burglar tools and collapsible paddle tossed in the bow, and frantically down these marble stairs toward a host of people veering out of the way, shouting, "Watch out, canoe— Heads up, canoe—Here comes a bloody canoe!" my heart doing its own soft shoe, any second expecting Mortlake's cry—and nearly decapitating a dowager, "My word, Aubrey!"—down this last slippery flight and right on by the sergeant-major whipping open the door and tipping his visored cap as I go striding up to the corner—Arab, of course, putting it to good use for those paddles up the Euphrates—and onto the back of this double-decker bus, knocking bowlers and monocles awry! "I say, what do you think you're doing?" that Indian conductor behind me, "Sir, this is not permitted—" and swinging round to confront him, fling him headlong into the street as we go roaring away and a flurry of people burst out of Harrods' door, arms waving, Mortlake and Hynde to the fore! Lowering my canoe and wedging up these narrow, winding stairs to the top deck—and into the open air! A sweet river breeze billowing my bedsheet and swiftly down the Brompton Road, leaving all that commotion behind!

Hagar

Flynn's silver Austin-Healey squealing up before Harrods with Ciara jouncing back in my lap—gripping her trim waist tight, "Thank you!"—and this chattering crowd, along with bobbies and reporters, milling about that dazed Indian conductor.

"What's going on?"

A photographer turning to me, "Some sheik just stole a canoe."

"Sheik—O Christ! Where'd he go?"

"Took off on a number 30 bus."

Flynn slam-shifting out onto Brompton Road, "Sure he's headed for the Thames!" whizzing ahead of this traffic, past the Victoria and Albert Museum and down Exhibition Road, grazing a passing cab—and a klaxon bleating somewhere, back there—a covey of pigeons fluttering white, scurrying gray, people dodging this way, that, bowler-hatted toff cursing after, and flat out into Cromwell Place toward an old woman in a polka-dot dress pedaling her two-speed bike—"*Flynn!*"—as she reins it up like a horse and we go zipping by, past this Church of Scotland, priest skipping the light fantastic, with Ciara's hand now clutching mine behind her and another klaxon joining the first, "Sure and they've got the entire flippin' Yard out now!" into the Fulham Road and Flynn switching on the radio, the BBC booming forth with traffic reports, weather reports, "—*The temperature currently*

22 degrees centigrade," down Sydney Street with him changing stations, "*—and ironically, tonight at nine, the Tate is presenting a private Gala Retrospective of Mr. Boyne's work—*" "*WHAT?!*" "*—though the artist himself is presumed drowned—*"

"There's definitely somethin' fishy here!"

"Flynn, over *there!*"

On the corner a cabbie in Arab burnoose shaking out a bedsheet—screeching tires round the curve of the U, horns loudly honking, and we jolt to a stop before him.

"Where'd ya get that outfit?"

"None of yer bleedin' business!"

Flynn hopping out to confront the cabbie with a fistful of cash, then back in a flash, "Seamus hadn't the fare, so he bartered his clothes instead," for another wheeling U-turn, "then was dropped with the canoe at the Thames!" and off we go again!

Boyne

Like bloody Hiawatha paddling deliriously down the river!—
starboard, port, God only knows! as I keep up this steady,
splashing pace against the current—and on under Chelsea
Bridge, staying close to the shore with the whole of London
pursuing me—and that tour boat passing by, tourists waving—
I'm waving, smiling back—always smile: Iraqi, of course, testing
it out for those paddles up the—no, that was my last disguise!
Just on vacation, off the reservation, over from Donegal trawling
for cod, ha-ha!—clad as I am now in Laetitia's lilac, Oscar
Wildelike blouse, my tan slacks, green-striped socks, and the
trusty beret—

"And Billy, as soon as I hang this portrait of Ciara, I'm
joining you and my ancestor, King of Ireland in the sixth century,
and farewell to the Celtic satyr!" under the blue arches of
Vauxhall Bridge toward that gray, shingled shore—"Least I won't
die arthritically like Renoir or blind like Mary Cassatt, be the
same age as my father, thirty-eight, Van Gogh at thirty-seven,
Modigliani at thirty-five—and all those wasted lives destroyed by
drink and suicide of *my* generation: Pollock mangled in a car
crash, David Smith in a truck crash, Arshile Gorky hanging

himself, Frank O'Hara, Franz Kline—as I go leaping out onto the beach with a crunching splash and, pushing the canoe back into this fast-moving current, skip up the river steps and on toward the Tate!

Hagar

Flynn's Healey careening across the honking Kings Road and left — grazing the curb — down Oakley Street, "Ah, but sure and Seamus is childlike, of course, knows no restraint — but ya shoulda seen him with that girl of his, Tory!" weaving in and out of taxis and between these red double-decker buses, "Granted, 'twas only over the short span, but still they were bloody marvelous together, never saw him happier than he was with her. O obsessed Boyne may be, but totally without malice, bringin' excitement and wonder into all our lives!" Ciara nodding (pining?) as we near the Thames — "Ah, but Jaysus, I just realized ya can't see a thing from the car along Chelsea Embankment, so I'll leave the two of ya here to search the river while I pop off to the Tate," past Cheyne Walk — Cadogan Pier down there — bumping onto the pavement, nicking the bollards, through these hedges — Ciara and I bounding out, stumbling, banging my knee — and Flynn turning to me, the klaxons growing louder, "Meet ya back at the townhouse at three!"

"OK — but listen, are any of Boyne's old lovers' husbands around?"

"Old lovers' husbands? Well there's Dungannon, of course."

"Dungannon?"

"O sure. Seamus had a fling with his wife — she was a flautist with Munich Bach Orchestra, who every night gave Percy the *St. Matthew Passion*, while his passion waned. Lasted a year, before she fled with her flaut. Even tried the rhythm method, only his was a jig and hers was a dirge."

"And where's Dungannon now?"

"Well I'm not quite certain meself, at Kew, most likely, in case Seamus, ya know, should return—" and, with two fangs of vapor shooting out his exhaust pipes, zooming away he goes!

Ciara and I walking rapidly along the Embankment under the deafening traffic's roar—and no sign of Boyne down there!—a tour boat gliding by, tug on the far side—"God, we're never gonna find him!"

"Gene?"

"What?" hurrying on ahead.

"You know you still haven't told me how he could paint me without ever seeing me."

"He said he painted you from my writings."

"Your writings? What did you write?"

"No, no, just some descriptions."

"Descriptions? Descriptions of what?"

"Physical, poetic descriptions of you, and he took it from there."

"I never knew I had that sort of effect."

"Well obviously you did," nearing Chelsea Bridge, "Christ, where the hell *is* he?" Still no sign of him, the wall higher here—on my toes, "I can't *see* all the way over!"

"So climb up."

"Up *there?*"

"Why not?"

"—I'm afraid of heights."

"All right, I'll go then."

"No way!" Ciara gracefully scaling it like a lithe, sensual cat—"Well just be careful!"

The tide of her hair lacing against the pale shine of her face, toedancing atop the parapet, using her arms as a balance, wobbling slightly, high above the Thames—

"See anything yet?"

"No, nothing as yet."

Her tight-fitting white sweatsuit snugly accentuating the sassy curves of her rump—and on her face, an expression I've never seen before: serene in this buffeting breeze, windlashing her blonde hair across her eyes, as I keep pacing anxiously below, "You're not afraid of the fall?"

"—Not at all."

"Christ, my greatest fear is acro—*Whoa*, watch it there!" grabbing onto her hand, "Acrophobia."

"Thank you—My God, what a view! You should *see*, Gene."

"I can see, I can see! Ciara, that's enough—"

"*Wait, wait!*" she leaning forward and to the side, "There's a *canoe* down there!"

Craning over the wall, "With Boyne *in* it?"

"No, there is no one in it—" her sneakers sliding, "—*Gene, hold me!*" fingers slipping out of my grip, windmilling her arms—

"*CIARA!!*"

—and headfirst she goes toppling off—

Christ Almighty!—disappearing from view—a distant splash!—as I go scrambling blindly onto the wall, no time for fears now!—and jumping straight out and holding my nose, falling fast, the Thames below coming up to meet me—exploding into the water! eyes popping, cheeks bulging, *Jesus*, I forgot I'm a lousy swimmer!—as I bounce gasping and blinking to the surface—and there's Ciara, already on shore! And I was gonna rescue her! Some hero, huh?—flailing hard against the current, and she helps me up onto this emergency pier.

Boyne

—And Good *God*, just *look* at that glorious, Victorian Tate! So damn excited, striding swiftly up Millbank and adjusting my dashing beret — all those blazing Turners inside! — that my hands are shaking, erection swaying, *Magnificat* echoing uproariously in my brain: *There was a young man from Iraq / Who played the bass viol with his cock / With tremendous erections / He rendered selections / From Johann Sebastian Bach!* Cézanne saying with an apple he'd astonish Paris, and soon they'll be saying — nay, surely huzzahing! — that with this radiant image of Ciara, I have astonished the entire world!

And strange, how I can't stop thinking of her: a sunburst obscuring the circling of gulls, fringing their wings with a border of gold —

O Jesus NO! Two bobbies patrolling the front — and spinning left down Atterbury Street, these black spoke fences, with my beret canted low — How the hell do I get *in*? Can't just pop in the front door, nowhere to hide. Have to secret myself somewhere till they're closed, all the guards've left — don't know how — these walls of Portland stone, grassy gardens, and vaulted basement windows — none ajar, metal bars — but I have to get in *now*, before I die or someone does me in! Staff entry down there, elderly guard with his froggy eyes, blue shirt, and black tie, leafing through his morning paper — while I'm passing by and pausing as he yawns, slowly standing, and goes waddling somewhere inside, his silhouette down the hall. Toward the loo? Looking left and right — the coast is clear — just say I'm Mr. O'Keefe from County Meath, needing to tap a kidney too —

And with a glide, I go sidling quickly indoors! Must be a loo along here, white-walled corridor — that toilet flushing, guard coming out! — *O Suffering Christ!* — and nipping sharply into the Ladies beside it!

"Hell*ooo?*" using my quavering Duchess falsetto — not a sound, glancing around — before locking myself in this stall! Another successful Irish crime: breaking into the Tate! (Though the reason the crime rate in Ireland's so low is 'cause nobody ever gets caught!)

Hagar

Ciara, having changed into Brenda's silky crimson robe, parading back and forth with her lithe and flowing stride, "Then what do you think happened to him?"

"God only knows, but I really doubt that he drowned."

"So do I," as she keeps on pacing.

"'Cause he was always a very good swimmer. And now the police're involved, dragging the river, all sorts of reporters, the Tate calling—it's suddenly become a *media* event!"

"Yes, and they don't even know him—but that also was a very brave thing *you* did, Gene."

"What?"

"Conquering your fear of heights to save me," Ciara's smiling bluestone eyes, "or let me save you," as she moves toward the rear, windowed wall.

"Right, well I think what we both need now is a shower, while our clothes're drying."

"Fine, fine."

"Where're you going?"

"I have to make a call," seating herself on an alcove cushion.

And I jog wetly up this short flight of stairs to the third floor and its black and white tiled bathroom with that green, fluffy

rug, hanging plants, and glass-enclosed shower stall. Peeling off
these sodden clothes and wrapping a towel around my waist—
make my move now or in a shower of sensual delights? This bar
of Yardley, temperature just right, soaping each other up, the
slippery feel of her firm wet flesh, lovely slope of her shoulders,
tracing round her nipples and coming closer as we kiss, gulping
kisses, under a hot steamy shower and kneeling down and lifting
her back against the tile with her arms about my neck as I thrust
deep inside, letting her slick skin slide—O everything falling
into place, the two of us growing closer, like Paris again—and I
go cantering down the stairs, by these worn and upholstered
chairs.

Ciara still on the phone, listening and nodding, "—Yes? O
you did, yes?" as she glances up, "No, no, I *do* understand,
Arthur. Yes, of course I do, I know you are still optimistic."

Whispering, "Who're you talking to?"

She whispering back, "(My agent.) No, of course not,
Arthur, and I will see you later then. Yes, yes, I am fine, thank
you, good-bye," sighing deeply now and averting her eyes.

"Did you get the part?"

Ciara standing and still blinking, "No, they gave it to the
producer's girl friend."

"O Jesus!" and smoothing back her hair, the silky shimmer
above her temples shading into a soft blonde shine, "I'm sorry,
really."

"Though now they may want me for another play—"

"Well whatever happens," gently holding her by the shoulders, "at least Ireland'll be incredible—"

"—even though it is only a small part—"

"—Can't wait to show you Carnaween, Boyne's twelve-
room house by the Irish Sea—"

"—Peter Brook now may be the director—"

"—Hell, you could even act at the Abbey, do Synge and
O'Casey—"

"—and Albert Finney supposedly is playing the lead—"

"—'cause one thing for sure, Ciara, I'm not going to lose
you again—"

"—and they need—'Lose me again'?"

"—finally start living our dream—"

"*What* dream, Gene? That I would run away with you as though I were nineteen again?"

"—'cause there's so much I want to show you—"

"But I hardly know you and you don't know me!"

"—all through Ireland and Dublin and of course Carnaween—"

"Gene, we knew each other seven years ago in Paris for how long, two or three weeks?"

"—follow the railroad tracks around to Kilcoole—"

"And it has never been *my* dream to go to Ireland, it has always been *your* dream to go to Ireland!"

"—meeting again like seven years never existed—"

"*Gene*," Ciara suddenly pushing my hands away, "you are not even *hearing* me now!"

"—finally take care of you—What're you *doing*?" bumping into the sofa.

"Well you have hardly heard a word I have said and you obviously have no *idea* what my life is like here, what I wish to *do* with my life, who I am!"

"What do you mean I have no *idea*? What're you *talking* about?"

"And maybe you can live your life just running away to Ireland or wherever, but I certainly cannot!"

"But we're *not* just running away, we're really going to *live* it now, 'cause everything's still the same—"

"But everything is *not* still the same, we have all changed!"

"No, not the way I feel about you! Nothing's changed except we can finally be with each other!"

"Gene, this is *your* fairy tale! I told you before I have had enough of being taken care of, of being rescued like Cinderella. Look, I have never been Cinderella and you have never been the prince!"

"But I've never been Milo, either!"

"No? Well you are certainly acting like someone who only hears himself!" moving past me round the room.

"So what'll you do," following after her, "just keep on acting?"

"Yes, I will do what I decided to do during my divorce."

"And what if you don't get this part?"

"I will get another one! I mean, who knows, it's possible I might not get a part until I am seventy-four, but I will go on trying."

"Ciara — ?"

"No, you don't understand what I'm saying, do you, or what I feel? You're blind to feelings, other people's feelings — "

"Blind? You once told me how sensitive I was — "

"Yes, but it is a special sort of sensitivity. That is, you perceive and you analyze what other people feel, but you never really feel in their place. You know what they feel, but you never really *feel* what they feel. You won't allow yourself — Even in your writing, you observe and you watch, but everything that I read in Paris was always a reflection of what *you* felt. There was never one character who felt for himself. And now here you are doing the same thing to me, and running again. Though I am not quite sure what you are running toward, Ireland and Joyce and me, all part of your fantasy to be a writer? If you want to be a writer, write! All you need is a pencil and paper!"

."And that's *it?*"

"Gene, I'm sorry I am being so harsh, because I do like you and I didn't want to hurt you."

"Didn't want to hurt me? Why didn't you say that seven *years* ago? For seven years, all I've thought about, dreamed of writing about was you — and now I've given up my wife, my business, my whole life back there — It's *never* been a fantasy! Never! Not when I described you to Boyne, then meeting here again, you and he running off together — And what *about* Boyne, how do you feel about him?"

Ciara glancing away, "I'm not sure yet how I feel — I just hope he is still alive."

Boyne

Darting fast looks left and right out of the ladies' loo—before skipping silently across the hall like a leprechaun or bearded Celtic satyr, my painting gripped in one hand, Aer Lingus bag in the other, using my sprinter's speed, real quick—footsteps sounding—*O Suffering Christ!*—and nipping round this corner, swiftly out of sight—my head in a dizzying whirl!

This sinister shadow approaching—Herr Mumble? IRA? Laura's hit man? Who? Fee, Fi, Fo, Fum, I smell the blood of an Irishmun—and a large, portly guard in a suit of indigo serge comes haarumphing into view, thumbs vested within his watch-fob pockets—*can't* get caught now that I've broken in!—he's lumbering left, I'm cringing right, pressing flat against the wall—as he vanishes, still haarumphing, down the hall, and I hear him say goodnight!

Letting out a sigh, must be after six by now—Tory and I once hiding out in the Baltimore Museum 'til they were closed, then slowly emerging to see it the only way you should, by flashlight and alone! And God, so missing her now! Such a beautiful girl with her blonde Swede hair—for every child's an artist, as Picasso said, the problem is how to remain an artist once you grow up! And the critics overlooking all the agonizing struggle and mental planning that goes into a work of art, the seemingly never-ending, nerve-rending shape and reshape, reflection, and study—"Though I painted up a bloody *storm*, didn't I, Billy, with my worn brushes and palette knife! frenzied fingers and 'eagle-talon' thumbnail like yours gouging, scratching, and scrubbing aurora yellow across a field of green—'til gradually and as if by magic that widening gyre of color turned into a wondrous Ciara (who's even better in reality!)—this work that'll never die!"

Outside, another driving rainstorm scudding over the Thames, those awaiting, darkling waves, while inside, there only remains this last act of hanging to do!

"And so few if any aware of what the artist goes through, denying our struggles during our lifetime and even recommending bloodletting for you, Billy, and a lobotomy for me to cure our diseased minds!" **"Aye, lad, took 'em 'til 1939 to find fifty of my greatest paintings in the cellars of the National Gallery, thought they were old tarpaulins!"** "O Christ, I know, the public forever losing sight of the man—Cézanne behind the apples and pears, on his deathbed calling out the name of the museum director who rejected his paintings, or you back of that whirling and radiant vortex, short and squat with your quizzical gray eyes, handsome beak of a nose, ruddy face, and rolling gait: a sexual rogue, never marrying, though seeking anonymity (even posing as 'Admiral Booth') to keep the demons at bay! Hell, remember the first time I heard you talking to me, it was here at the Tate, all gruff and thundering in your deep basso voice: 'My paintings are my children!'"

Good *God*, what a life! Leaving everything behind me now, Tory, Ciara, Sligo, my father, dying in that Rhode Island asylum. Loved to see him whipping up his own special béchamel sauce, velouté or mornay, under his framed photo of Escoffier, and that astounding Hong Kong curry, served in infinite varieties of mild, medium, and blast your bloody head off! Finally sneaking some in, rather than that psychiatric gruel, the night before he died and sharing his last meal with him—O my father! same face as mine, though smaller and Van Gogh-eyed. But Christ, we're *all*

fathers, and you don't love anyone *but* yourself if you're afraid to
love your father! Memories galore, Erin's green and fragrant
shore —

And that first morning of land, the gulls cawing madly,
balanced as they were on air, then swooping down the long slide
and back to their tentative, poised hover. Spontaneously a thin
sliver of earth out of the pitching sea, a lighthouse winking:
Ireland. Green slice in a graygreen sea and I was so excited to be
returning again, ten years after his funeral, drunk and awake all
night with the gulls spearing my stale bits of cake that I let out a
wild call from the side rail, my free fist pumping the air and
shouting, "God bless Ireland!" while I pointed my erection
toward solid land, "There're only two countries left in all this
barbarous woe — Ireland and Israel — and they'll fight it out
between 'em!" when tiny, heeled feet began descending the
stairway above, a white, pleated skirt coming slowly into view as I
spun about, hard-on in tow. She blinked. A startled gasp. She
paused. Then fled up the stairs in the wake of my laughter — and
two months later she became my wife!

O Laura, what a bewitching summer that was, no money
nor cares, just living on air with my Sarah Lawrence grad, posing
bare for my paintings again and again (but still so far from Ciara's
vision of ripeness and bloom!) as I chased you round my studio!
Or making love atop that hill in Kilcoole after watching a herd
of ponies woo one another, nuzzling about and running down
a glade with such exquisite freedom and ease, and a month
later, when you found you were pregnant, you couldn't remember our lovemaking at all or where Tory was conceived, just those
ponies running along — Sweet Jesus, taking my newborn babe
in my arms and humming "Sleepers Awake" — O *Tory*, the pain
of your loss — tearing you from me — disappearing into the
abyss!!

More footsteps sounding — cane tapping? Herr Mumble,
Mündel? — and holding my breath, making myself invisible!

That froggy little guard, a rotund toad with his bulging eyes,
hardly pausing as he waddles by and tapping the floor with a
pointer!

Irish Wine

Waiting a few moments more, then scampering into this darkened kitchen, everyone gone for the day, and sneaking a look outside. Only when it falls suddenly past the dark, soaked wood, do you see it: pale rain falling into sight, the leaves a wet and smoky green. Gray aftermath of rain, gurgling down the gutters or lacing the windows with intricate webs and woven designs. Those bobbies still there, guards departing—and the doors clanging closed with an echoing slam!

I'm all alone in the Tate!!

Ha-ha!! tingling in me bones as I cant my dashing beret, tuck in this lilac blouse and head back the way I came, swiftly past the staff entrance and trotting up these empty stairs, not a sound and turning around—

Suffering CHRIST!! Light *bursting* out of darkness: *Sunrise, Snow Storm, Venice Skies, Self-Portrait*—

"Billy, I'm naked to the *core* before you! For to come upon your work again is surely to forget death and time with this *splendor* of seething light! And now *HERE!!*" unfurling my one surviving gem—O Ciara, to hold you once more and love you just as you are! *Golden haired and golden hearted/I would ever have you be,/As you were when last we parted/Smiling slow and sad at me*—and raising it high, "Billy, I'm finally going to hang *beside* you! For as you can see, like you, I'm even a better lover on canvas—though with Ciara I've never been so tender and passionate and lyrically warm! Such a shame it'll all end like this, during torrential showers and the floodtide, ebbtide of Old Father Thames, that ancient, silty river!"

Opening my Aer Lingus bag and sifting through cold cream, stain, manila rope—Ah, my Harrods hammer, and taking it out along with these ha'penny nails. No frame, charred round the edges—Just have to bang it into a wall. But where's that marvelous spot? By your *Snow Storm* or *Sunrise?* Or what about round this corner? Strolling toward the main hall, these green curtains drawn. Wonder why? Peeking inside—

"*GOOD GOD!!!*"

And come face-to-face with my work—*ALL* of my work, old and new! *Must* be a mirage! Blinking, rubbing my eyes, and gazing in staggering amazement: No, it's true! *Everything* I thought was burned now before me on the walls!

And this accompanying brochure—

Tonight at nine
A Private Gala Retrospective
of the Works of Seamus Boyne

—printed a month ago! as I fling it high in the air, "O those *bastards!* Well I'll give 'em a show!"

Hagar

"Gene? Ciara? Anybody about?"

"Yeah, we're up here," glancing uneasily at her as Flynn, with his orange curls and mustache, comes trotting up the stairs, along with Laetitia, Dungannon and his pipes, "Any news?"

"Well we still haven't got a clue about Boyne, but the Tate's paid the ransom to the IRA—"

"The *IRA*? What the hell's going *on*?"

"—though Percy here's been doing some diggin', and 'tis high time we had us a bit of a natter with Vi and Brenda—"

"Vi and Brenda, why?"

"Well it seems that—" Those two phones shrilly ringing and Flynn bounding over to grab one, "What? No, Mr. Boyne hasn't been 'found as yet'! Yer like vultures waitin' to pounce!" then slamming it down, "More of them bloody reporters!" The phone ringing again and Flynn bellowing into it, "Will ya for Jaysus' sake go 'way—Arson, is it? Police draggin' the river? O by the crucified fuckin' Christ!" and slamming it down once more.

"Shhh!" Ciara holding up her hand.

"What?"

"I thought I heard—Yes, there it is again. Did you hear that?"

Everybody listening intently, looking around.

"Sounds like shouting, a man's voice, coming from the gallery."

"But the fire, why would anyone—?"

"Let's go!" Flynn leading the way quickly down the dark corridor into this bare, lattice-windowed room, still acrid with smoke—then pulling up short with bated breath, "Jaysus, I'd know that voice anywhere!"

"It's Vi, screaming at someone down there!"

"—Confounded Ordway, you're becoming increasingly senile these days!"

All of us whispering, "*Ordway?*" "The butler did it?" "What did he say?" "Shhhh, just listen!"

"—and both of us know you don't deserve a penny—"

"But, m-madam, I only want what's rightfully mine."

"—since it was you and your bumbling Sinn Féin mates who caused this dreadful fire—"

"Jaysus!"

"—by knocking over those candlestands—"

"Scandal, m-madam? But you said the Tate paid the ransom and he drowned all by himself—"

"O those bloody *hags!*" and Flynn about to go charging down the stairs, "I'm gonna tear their arms right out of their sockets!"

"*No!*"

"*No?* Why the hell *not?*"

"'Cause they could lead us to Boyne—"

"Shhh, listen!"

"—but we'll settle this matter later, because now we must leave for the Tate."

And off they go, a taxi waiting outside.

"Come on!"

Down through the still smoking ruins of the gallery, doddering old Ordway, in his blue butler's suit, climbing slowly into the front of the cab, Vi and Brenda in back, as we all hop in: Flynn and Dungannon on the jumpseats, Laetitia up with Ordway, and Ciara and I on either side of the sisters.

"Pardon me, ladies, but I'm sure ya won't mind if the lot of us share yer ride? Frightful London traffic, ya know?"

"*What?* — How dare you! What is the meaning of this? And Laetitia, what are you — ?"

The driver pulling away.

"And I wonder now might we ask ya a few questions?"

" — Questions? — Why, what sort of questions?" Vi's terrified rhino face as Brenda keeps cowering beside her.

"Vi, you said no one would — "

"Brenda, *not* now! Driver, pull over this instant! This man is out of his mind!"

"Well our investigations have shown that you'd acquired considerable debts due to yer father's financial extravagance — "

"Sheer nonsense!"

" — and, therefore, devised this devilish scheme just after Sligo did himself in!"

"Driver, I demand — "

Dungannon glaring at the stubby driver, who continues silently steering.

" — knew ya'd receive no immediate rewards for the Retrospective, so ya guaranteed the Tate the old work, then stole the new work yerselves and offered it back for ransom!"

"And worst of all, tried to kill Boyne so his paintings'd become invaluable!"

"*Exactly*, Gene!"

"Vi, is this true?"

"We demand to speak to our solicitor! *Driver?*" Vi raising her riding crop —

"Solicitor! I'll give ya a bloody solicitor, ya whore's melt you!" and Flynn, swiping the riding crop out of her hand, is about to rain blows upon her head — when Dungannon yanks it from him, holding him at bay.

Flynn still pawing and kicking, "Will ya let *go* of me! They're worse than Goneril and Regan, they are!"

The taxi racing past Vauxhall Bridge and there's the Tate shimmering in violet light, bobbies ringing the fences, as we come wheeling down Atterbury Street, lined with shiny limos, Jaguars and Rollses, and swerve to a screeching halt.

"Yes, well I'm terribly sorry now that we can't discuss this further—Come, Brenda—"

"Yer not goin' *anywhere!*"

"—since we're already late as it is."

Flynn still clawing at her, "Jaysus, Gene, yer not gonna let 'em *go!*"

"No, we'll just escort them in."

Vi sliding by me, with Brenda alongside fluttering her boa, Ordway still muttering about "scandals," and the rest of us, Dungannon shouldering his bagpipes, right behind.

"How're *we* gonna get in?"

"Just follow along," Laetitia displaying a card, "they are with me," past the security guards, TV crews, a battery of press and photographers, and under the statue of Britannia, self-conscious now in my Irish sweater and Adidas sneakers, raking my fingers through my hair, Ciara in her tight white sweat-suit—and inside the main hall, long tables of hors d'oeuvres and cocktails against the wall, and around a hundred formally dressed people seated before those dark green curtains, Vi and Brenda hurrying down to the front row as I rest my hands on Ciara's shoulders—letting me hold her, relaxing under my grasp—But hold who? (*You obviously have no idea what my life is like here, what I wish to do with my life, who I am!*) Losing her again? But how can I lose her if I never really had her? More than words and paintings—All part of my fantasy to be a writer! (*If you want to be a writer, write! All you need is a pencil and paper.*) But write about what? More dreams, romantic illusions? Or the reality of them and me? Joyce fleeing through flung nets past the pain of Ireland to write about what he knew. But what did he know in Paris, Zurich, and Trieste but himself, Ireland, his father. And here I've come all this way to write the story of my father, Great Neck, and the world I grew up in? (*Longest way round is the shortest way home!*) And the one way I have to really understand him (and maybe myself), though now he'll never read my work—as Laetitia keeps pointing out who's who: "That is Princess Margaret, of course, with Philippe de Rothschild, Francis Bacon, Armand Hammer is over there—" "*Quiet*, please!" "—and that is Kenneth Clark who is talking!"

"—Several years ago at Mr. Boyne's initial show, I shared with numerous others the feeling that here, in fact, was a talent of remarkable promise, an imagination absolutely vehement in its personal logic, in its determination to summarize all experience in the rhythmic flow of a swirl of pigment. Those splendid blazing outbursts served to remind us once again of the seduction and relish of visual language. He offered us then the possibilities of passionate commitment—someone willing to risk and to fail, someone willing to feel and to care, and finally, someone, now brilliantly fulfilled, I feel safe this evening in calling clearly the greatest artist of the twentieth century—"

"O just open the bloody curtains already before my *arms* fall off!"

HIS voice back there?! But how the hell could he—?

And a totally stunned Clark, fumbling and jerking the curtains apart, reveals a manically grinning Boyne standing naked (except for his beret, fig leaf, and those green-striped socks) with his arms outstretched like a crucified Christ or hung painting in the center of his stolen work as he comes leaping down from a pedestal amid a pandemonium of shrieking and screaming, women fainting, cameras flashing, and shouting as he goes, "Good *God*, you Yahoos still haven't learned, have you, that there's never art without the artist!" Flynn breaking into rousing song, Dungannon's bagpipes bleating, "*All you free-born men of the travelling people—*" and bare-assed Boyne now bowing with a flourishing sweep before a gaping Princess Margaret—as Ciara goes rushing out of my grasp—reaching after her, *gone!*—and through the crowd to hug him and hold him, "Ah *Christ*, Billy, and here's my inspiration in the flesh!" kissing her wildly, "who just wants me to be!" and they go dancing away out the door to the echoing Irish music.

Taking another deep breath, my gut aching, as I watch them leave, and Laetitia, following, turns to me, "Are you coming, Gene?"

"No—I think it's time to go home."

"To Ireland?"

"No, *there* goes Ireland, home to New York."

Chinua Achebe
Anthills of the Savannah £3.95

'A tremendous work, and a brave one' LITERARY REVIEW

'A work in which 22 years of harsh experience, intellectual growth,
self-criticism, deepening understanding and mustered discipline of skill open
wide a subject to which Achebe is now magnificently equal'
NADINE GORDIMER

It is the troubled present in West Africa. Two years after the military coup that
swept a brilliant young Sandhurst-trained army officer to power there is an
uneasy calm in the state of Kangan. His Excellency, defeated in a vital
referendum, nervous and embittered, finds comfort in the role of dictator.
For those who helped him to power, his oldest friends, the future looks
dangerous and uncertain. Chris Oriko, Minister of Information, and Ikem
Osodi, poet and editor – innocent when the blood-letting begins – are forced
to become players in a drama of love and friendship, betrayal and death, that
mirrors the history of their troubled country.

'Achebe's four previous novels earned him the title of Africa's greatest
novelist, and nothing has happened since to detract from that . . . This book
brings humanity to a world in which we feared it did not exist'
RICHARD DOWDEN, THE INDEPENDENT

'In a powerful fusion of myth, legend and modern styles, Achebe has written
a book which is wise, exciting and essential' FINANCIAL TIMES

'Achebe's achievement is write honestly about 30 years of pain and
disillusionment and still see hope for the future in simplicity and goodness.
I found the novel exciting, informative and very wise; an altogether
marvellous book' DAILY TELEGRAPH

'Achebe's most complex, enigmatic and impressive work yet'
NEW STATESMAN

'A masterly *tour de force*, written with elegance, irony and hope'
THE GUARDIAN

William Burroughs
Queer £2.95

'A major work. Burroughs' heart laid bare' ALLEN GINSBERG

His legendary and most revealing novel, published at last after three decades, *Queer* is a strikingly candid and powerful work which takes the reader back into the homosexual underworld of the forties and into the very core of Burroughs' unique sensibiity.

Queer is a love story – the account of William Lee's painfully circular seduction of Eugene Allerton in Mexico City, and the romantic agonies he suffers. In his introduction Burroughs discusses frankly and courageously the shattering event that happened after the occurrences described in *Queer*, and how this event has haunted his life and affected his work.

'A major work . . . The love story is told with astonishing economy, Burroughs conjuring the heights and the depths in an intensely lyrical shorthand which seems to imitate and not travesty feeling' SUNDAY TIMES

'The Mexico it depicts is phosphorescent and the portrait of William Lee is devastating. For William Burroughs, start here' NEW STATESMAN

'Shocking the world all over again, Burroughs has written a thoughtful and sensitive study of unrequited love . . . Retroactively the book humanises his work' MARTIN AMIS, OBSERVER

'A vividly evoked depiction of frustration and obsession; human, richly comic, strangely touching, . . . well worth waiting for' GAY TIMES

'A blueprint for many of Burroughs' themes, narrative techniques and characterizations, it helps us come to grips with the dark humour, violent energy and unsettling vision of this writer who has forced himself into our consciousness and seized a place in literary history' NEW YORK TIMES BOOK REVIEW

'The only American novelist living today who may conceivably be possessed by genius' NORMAN MAILER

Bruce Chatwin
The Songlines £3.99

'I have a vision of the Songlines stretching across the continents and ages; that wherever men have trodden they have left a trail of song; and that these trails must reach back, in time and space, to an isolated pocket in the African savannah, where the First Man shouted the opening stanza of the World song, "I am!"'

'The Songlines emerge as invisible pathways connecting up all over Australia; ancient tracks made of songs which tell of the creation of the land. The aboriginal's religious duty is ritually to travel the land, singing the Ancestors' songs: singing the world into being afresh. *The Songlines* is one man's impassioned song' SUNDAY TELEGRAPH

'This is a stunning work. From the author of *In Patagonia*, it is . . . a personal quest into the nature of knowledge. Totally absorbing and stimulating' THE GOOD BOOK GUIDE

'He is such a fine and original writer. A white nomad himself, Chatwin's affinity with the footloose tribes of the endless outback yields one of the most affectionate portraits yet of a race ravaged by the alcohol that so many other Australians privately hope will become a self-administered final solution' DAILY MAIL

'Chatwin is not simply describing another culture; he is also making cautious assertions about human nature. Towards the end of his life Sartre wondered why people still write novels; had he read Chatwin's he might have found new excitement in the genre' EDMUND WHITE in THE SUNDAY TIMES

'The poetry of Chatwin's remarkable pages flitters quietly about, steering a course between William Blake and Dr Johnson . . . a masterpiece' JOHN BAILEY, LONDON REVIEW OF BOOKS

Bret Easton Ellis
Less Than Zero £2.95

The book that inspired the cult film

Set in affluent Los Angeles, *Less Than Zero* is a raw and powerful portrayal of a young generation that has experienced sex, drugs, and disaffection at too early an age. The narrator, Clay, returns home to Los Angeles for Christmas, but his holiday turns into a dizzying spiral of desperation that takes him through the rich suburban homes, the relentless parties, the seedy bars and the glitzy rock clubs. Morally barren, ethically bereft and tinged with implicit violence, *Less Than Zero* is the shocking coming-of-age novel about the casual nihilism that comes with youth and money.

'Bret Ellis is undoubtably the new master of youthful alienation. With spare, seamless writing he tells us a tale of collegiate Christmas in LA that makes Jack Kerouac and his Beat Generation seem like pussies. A harrowing yet poignant indictment of our times that is like a long day's journey into the LA night.' EMILY PRAGER, author of *A Visit from the Footbinder*

'This is the novel your mother warned you about. Jim Morrison would be proud.' EVE BABITZ, author of *Slow Days, Fast Company* and *La Woman*

'An extraordinarily accomplished first novel.'
THE NEW YORKER

Tama Janowitz
Slaves of New York £3.99

'If there were a literary equivalent to a new *Talking Heads* album, *Slaves of New York* would be that book' MADEMOISELLE

'Tama Janowitz is a clever writer. She draws trendy New York popartsies to a T. These New Yorkers are slaves to high rents, migratory relationships and, most significantly, their own contagious modishness . . . Janowitz's imagination is vivid and she can invent truly memorable situations and details . . . (She) can be laugh-out loud funny and wonderfuily sharp . . . A talented writer' WASHINGTON POST

'So savagely witty, so acerbic, so piercingly accurate . . . Tama Janowitz has a merciless eye for absurdity which she trains primarily on Greenwich Village "artistes". She traps them in self-conscious postering and serves them up as metaphors for her sardonic and quirky view of *au courant* urban life' LOS ANGELES HERALD EXAMINER

'Janowitz is a fearless writer. Her details are quirky, her language is lean, and her sentences sprint along with deceptive ease. The protagonists in her stories share with her a shyness and a sense of always being out of place. Although they try in earnest to fit in, they put on the wrong clothes or say the wrong thing or fail to grasp the subtle messages other people send their way . . . With the publication of *Slaves of New York*, Tama Janowitz could become the most talked-about writer of the year' NEW YORK

With the younger generation of writers already buried under a mound of volcanic hype, it is remarkable that Janowitz, unsmothered by critical acclaim for her novel *American Dad*, can write with such freshness' ELLE

'The shrewd observation, the skewed invention . . . are the gifts of a singular talent' JAY MCINERNEY, author of BRIGHT LIGHTS, BIG CITY, in the NEW YORK TIMES

Patrick O'Connor
Down the Bath Rocks £2.95

The scene is the Ardrossan slums of the 1920s. — the days of the horse
drawn cabs and bakers' carts, of serge suits and satin drawers. The cast —
Patrick O'Connor and his large Irish immigrant family who, like his friends, live
crowded together in a miserable attic, dependent for survival on occasional
labour and the pawn shop.

Through the boy's eyes we see the dimensions of his world slowly expanding
and his observations hardening as he grows older. The centre of his curiosity
gradually shifts from the strange and ever-present rituals of death, school and
religion to the terrifying mystery of sex and the nightmare of confession.
Through his eyes also we see with extraordinary and affectionate clarity the
numerous characters that people his world and the desperately deprived
environment in which they live — but by which they are never defeated.

Down the Bath Rocks is a major novel which will attract and hold readers of
every generation; as a re-creation of the working-class ethos of fifty years ago
it has few rivals; as a chronicle of a boy's struggle to maturity it has a vivid,
compulsive and sensitive honesty.

All these books are available at your local bookshop or newsagent, or can be ordered direct from the publisher. Indicate the number of copies required and fill in the form below.

Send to: **CS Department, Pan Books Ltd., P.O. Box 40, Basingstoke, Hants.   RG21 2YT.**

or phone: 0256 469551 (Ansaphone), quoting title, author and Credit Card number.

Please enclose a remittance* to the value of the cover price plus: 60p for the first book plus 30p per copy for each additional book ordered to a maximum charge of £2.40 to cover postage and packing.

*Payment may be made in sterling by UK personal cheque, postal order, sterling draft or international money order, made payable to Pan Books Ltd.

Alternatively by Barclaycard/Access:

Card No. ☐☐☐☐☐☐☐☐☐☐☐☐☐☐☐☐☐

Signature:

Applicable only in the UK and Republic of Ireland.

While every effort is made to keep prices low, it is sometimes necessary to increase prices at short notice. Pan Books reserve the right to show on covers and charge new retail prices which may differ from those advertised in the text or elsewhere.

NAME AND ADDRESS IN BLOCK LETTERS PLEASE:

....

Name————————————————————————————

Address———————————————————————————

————————————————————————————————

————————————————————————————————

————————————————————————————————

3/87